Mira went cautiously, alert for the sound of hooves or marching feet. She was just beginning to breathe more easily when she saw the glimmering mist gathering over the road ahead of her. She stopped and watched, rooted to the spot, as the mist thickened and bulged into arms and a head with hollow, staring eyes and a dark circle of a mouth—but nothing more, only darkness for features. It was raw energy, a specter gathered, but still unformed, a wild ghost, a thing seeking form and purpose. Its kind were the most dangerous sort of phantoms, for they were voracious.

It shot toward her, moaning, and her heart leaped into her throat . . .

BOOKS BY CHRISTOPHER STASHEFF

CHRISTOPHER STASHEFF

A WIZARD IN THE WAY

TOR®
fantasy

A TOM DOHERTY ASSOCIATES BOOK
NEW YORK

This is a work of fiction. All the characters and events portrayed in this book are either products of the author's imagination or are used fictitiously.

A WIZARD IN THE WAY

Copyright © 2000 by Christopher Stasheff

Edited by Jenna A. Felice

A Tor Book
Published by Tom Doherty Associates, LLC
175 Fifth Avenue
New York, NY 10010

www.tor.com

Tor® is a registered trademark of Tom Doherty Associates, LLC.

ISBN: 0-812-54168-5

First edition: September 2000
First mass market edition: November 2001

Printed in the United States of America

0 9 8 7 6 5 4 3 2 1

1

Someone hammered on the back door of the hut. Mira turned from the cookpot over the hearth and opened it, instantly worried—who was ill now?

Little Obol stood there, panting, eight years old, eyes wide with alarm. "Run, Mira! There are soldiers coming toward your house, and one has a parchment in his fist!"

Mira's heart lurched; dread weighted all her limbs. It had come at last. She gave the boy a sad smile. "There's no sense in running, Obol. If the magician wants one of his people, we've no choice but to go to him."

"You can flee!"

"Yes, to have his dogs sniff me out and his soldiers drag me back to him. No, I think I'd rather go with my head high and my clothes clean. But thank you, lad. Run along home, now— we don't want them to know you've been telling tales."

She bent and kissed his cheek. Obol blushed; he may have been only eight, but Mira was very pretty.

Too pretty for her own good, Mira thought with a sigh as she closed the door. By the time she was thirteen, it was clear that the pretty child was going to become a beautiful woman—but her parents had warned her that Magician Lord Roketh would command her to his bed if she were beautiful, and Mira suddenly understood why the prettiest girls in the village wept as they went to the castle with the soldiers. She had thought it would be a fine life, living in the lord's keep to cook or clean instead of doing the same work in a peasant hut all her life. Now, though, she understood why, when the girls came back to the village to buy food or cloth for their master, they seemed either timorous and fragile or hard and brazen. She vowed it would never happen to her and took pains to hide her beauty, tying her hair back in a severe bun and staying out in the sun so that her face would become tanned. She practiced looking spiritless and glum, only letting her natural cheerfulness bubble up at home.

It had worked well for years, but as she turned eighteen, even the dimmest eye could see how exquisite she had become, and her magician lord Roketh was anything but blind.

As were his soldiers. A fist pounded at the door. Quickly, Mira twisted her hair into a bun, secured it with a bone pin, then hurried to open the door, squinting against the sun. She didn't need to, but anything that made her look less attractive would help.

Four of Roketh's guards stood outside, grim in their leather and iron. "Mira, daughter of Howell?" their leader asked.

"I—I am she." Mira tried to make her voice sound gravelly.

"You are summoned to Lord Roketh, maiden. You will present yourself at the castle tomorrow in your best skirt and blouse."

"Yes . . . yes, sir."

"We shall come to accompany you, maiden. Be ready." With no more ceremony than that, the guard turned, barked a command to his fellows, and led them away.

Mira closed the door, trembling inside. She might be a

maiden when she went to the castle, but only for a day. She wondered how unpleasant that taking would be, then remembered Roketh's seamed old face, his glittering eye, the touch of cruelty in his smile as he rode through the village, and shuddered at the thought. She went to a curtain, lifted a corner, peered up at the castle that brooded over the town, and shuddered again. The gray stone pile was a fearsome place of sudden gouts of fire and crackling thunderbolts. Worse, Roketh himself was ugly and malicious, using his knowledge of healing to bribe and threaten, using his other magical powers to intimidate.

Mira remembered the neighbor who had not been able to pay his taxes one year because the labor Roketh demanded on his fields had left the family with no time to cultivate their own garden. The thatch of their cottage had burst into flame in the middle of the night. They had all come running out—they were all alive—but they'd had to watch everything they owned burn to the ground.

Then there was old Ethel, who had sworn a curse against Roketh when he had taken her daughter. Ethel's cow had gone dry the next day. Her pig had sickened and died, and her hens had lost their feathers and ceased laying. The next year, of course, she had not been able to pay her taxes, either.

Those she had known of her own witness, but there were many other tales: a man who had refused to go out to Roketh's fields because his wife was sick abed and their child too small to be left alone had seen his own garden wilt and die. Another had refused to let his daughter answer Roketh's summons and had died of a strange and disfiguring ailment. Soldiers who displeased Roketh were likely to have their own weapons turn upon them. None in her village had ever been rousted from their pallets in the middle of the night by terrifying, groaning, sharp-fanged ghosts, but she had heard of many who had, if their masters were ghost-leaders.

Mira knew her beauty would not last long if she dared defy Roketh. On the other hand, she had seen what a night spent with him had done to the other maidens who had been ordered to his bed, and when he finally sent them home, grown too old to interest him, they were drained of all enthusiasm, turned into dull-eyed, spiritless drudges. Any questions about what the magician had done to them evoked only cries of terror and floods of tears. Rumor said they woke screaming from nightmares.

What could Mira do? On the one hand, she was terrified at the thought of the ordeal the other maidens must have endured. On the other hand, she didn't want her parents or family to have to suffer hauntings, night-terrors, or madness from having tried to protect her.

There was one other choice. She would probably be captured and brought back in shame, but she had to risk it. The soldiers would not come until the next day, so that night, Mira slipped out the door and stole into the woods with a pack of travel rations.

The forest was gloomy and filled with terrifying sounds, but she dared not hide and wait for dawn—she must be as far away as possible before Roketh could learn she was missing and send his soldiers searching for her. She could not have fled during the day, of course, or the soldiers would have been on her trail immediately—but oh, the night was terrifying! Thoughts of wolves and bears made her steps drag and the occasional moan that might have come from a ghost sped her heels amazingly. Thus, now running, now creeping, Mira made her way through the lightless forest with her heart in her throat and a prayer on her lips.

The peasant paused to lean on his short-handled hoe, gazing off into the distance, his stare so vacant it was hard to believe he was seeing anything. His legs were wrapped in rough cloth cross-gartered to hold it in place; his shoes were wooden. The man's only other garment was a tunic of coarse cloth. His mouth lolled open, his forehead was low, his hair a black thatch.

Then a better-dressed man with boots and a sheepskin jacket, bearing a cudgel, came by and barked at the peasant. With a sigh, the man lowered his gaze again and set himself once more to chopping weeds.

Alea couldn't hear his voice, of course—the picture had been taken from orbit, and though light may travel twenty thousand miles, sound waves have more limited range. She turned to Gar—well, Magnus, really, but she would always think of him as Gar—and said, "Bad enough, but I've seen worse. In fact, I've *lived* through worse."

"So have I," Gar agreed. "This planet can wait. You must have more extreme cases on file, Herkimer."

"Of course, Magnus," the ship's computer answered. "How extreme would you wish?"

"The worst first."

"The worst is thirty light-years distant, Magnus, and there are two lesser cases on the way."

"If they're lesser," Alea said, "they don't need us."

"Let's look anyway," Magnus said. "If the worst is dreadful, the lesser cases may be horrid. We might not be able to bring ourselves to pass them by."

"Oh, all right," Alea said with a martyred sigh. "Which hard case is closest?"

They sat in the sybaritic lounge of Magnus's spaceship *Herkimer,* computer and ship being so tightly interlocked that it would be impossible to tell the difference. They sat on deeply cushioned chairs that molded themselves to the contours of their bodies as they shifted positions. Between them was a slab of jade on legs of porphyry, and if the substances weren't strictly natural, only an electron microscope could tell. Around them stretched deep-piled carpet of a dark red. The walls were lost in shadow except for pictures lighted by camouflaged lamps, as were their two chairs. All the rest was hidden in scented gloom. Mozart played softly from hidden speakers.

Alea twisted, feeling guilty at such luxury when people dwelt in the squalor pictured before them in midair, seeming as real as though the people and landscapes were actually before them in the room.

"These are the people of Beta Taurus Four," Herkimer told them.

Alea found herself staring at a circle of men and women wearing only loincloths and halters, bent low over the spokes of a turnstile that turned a mill wheel. An overseer in a leather jerkin and high boots stood watching, whip in hand. Behind him, oxen wandered, grazing.

"There are far more people than cattle on this planet," Herkimer told them, "so the men and women labor while the oxen grow fat to provide tender meat for the lords' banquets. There are fifteen hundred rulers and a million serfs, with twelve thousand overseers and supervisors to keep them healthy enough to work and drive them to exhaustion."

Alea shuddered. "Worse than the last by far." She turned to Magnus. "Where did Herkimer find this information?"

"My father's robot downloaded it into him." Magnus tried not to think about the details of family and self that Fess had downloaded with it. "My father is an agent for SCENT, the Society for the Conversion of Extraterrestrial Nascent Totalitarianisms. After Terra managed to throw off PEST, the Proletarian Eclectic State of Terra, the reactionary government that cut off the frontier planets, SCENT surveyed those colony worlds to see how they had fared during their centuries of isolation. They smuggled in agents who traveled wherever they could, taking pictures with hidden cameras. When their ships picked them up and brought them back to SCENT headquarters, they filed these pictures along with reports of what they had seen." He shrugged. "PEST lost quite a few records of which planets had been colonized, and later explorers have happened upon some of them." He didn't mention that his own home world had been one.

"So there may still be a great number left out there?"

Magnus nodded. "To be truthful, no one knows how many. During the last century of colonization, a host of disaffected groups scraped together enough money to buy and equip their own colony ships and went plunging off into the galaxy to try to find habitable planets. Some sent back reports, some didn't. SCENT assumes a large proportion of those last have died out."

"But some of them survived?"

"Survived, and don't want to be found—or at least, their founders didn't. Some of the groups who set out from Terra to found their own ideas of an ideal society were careful not to let anyone know where they were going. Others meant to but were rather careless. We don't know which colonies survived and which didn't."

Alea shuddered. "But we can't do anything about them, can we?"

"Not unless we happen upon one accidentally, no."

"And we have no idea what they're like?"

"Well, we know they haven't developed interstellar travel, or we would have heard from them," Magnus said. "Other than that, we only know that some of the ones we've found have developed very bizarre cultures."

Alea thought about what "bizarre" could mean and hid another shudder. The dread made her a bit more acerbic. "If you people in SCENT know—"

"Not me," Magnus said quickly, eyes on the scene before him. "I resigned."

Alea frowned; it was the first he had mentioned of ever

having belonged to his father's organization. She needed to follow that up, find out why he had joined and, even more, why he had quit—but she could see from his face that the time wasn't right. Instead, she went on. "All right, *those* people in SCENT. If they know lords are oppressing serfs on so many worlds, why don't they do something about it?"

"Because there *are* so many worlds," Magnus explained. "There are simply too many of them for SCENT to deal with all at once. After all, they have limited personnel, becoming more limited all the time as the old rebels who first staffed it die off or retire."

"So who's going to take care of the colonies they haven't reached yet?" Alea demanded.

"We will." Magnus flashed her a grin.

Alea stared. Then, slowly, she smiled back.

"Alert!" the computer's voice said. "I have just received a television signal."

"Television?" Magnus turned back toward the display area, tense as a leashed hound. "In H-space?"

"I can detect it, but I cannot receive it," Herkimer said. "Shall I drop into normal space and read it?"

"Please do so!"

Alea didn't understand the terms yet, but she wholeheartedly agreed with the sentiment. There was no feeling of a change in motion—the ship's internal gravity saw to that—but suddenly a woman and two men stood before them dressed in garish clothing. Behind them was an array of flashing lights and screens with abstract patterns. The woman had tears in her eyes and was trying to push her way between the men, who glared at each other as though ready to spring into a fight to the death. The colors kept blurring and bleaching, though, and the whole picture kept breaking into a sea of colored dots that lost their hues, then regained them, managing to pull together into the image again.

"The signal is very faint," Herkimer said. "I shall have to digitize and process it to make it consistent."

"Do so, please," Magnus said. "What is its source?"

"Extrapolating vector," Herkimer said, then a few seconds later, "There is no recorded planet in that vicinity."

"No *recorded* planet?" Gar turned to meet Alea's eyes, and the same thought rang in both minds: *Lost colony!*

Arnogle waited until the last glimmer of dusk had faded from the meadow, then came forth from the forest and stretched his arms upward, palms out. The tall cone of his hat pointed backward; his white beard and blue robe ruffled in the breeze, making the golden symbols embroidered there dance and ripple. Arnogle had told Blaize again and again that stretching the arms wasn't necessary to call ghosts but did help a man direct his thoughts toward them. It was only a trick, a technique, but Arnogle needed every bit of skill he could muster.

Only one or two ghosts came in answer to his summons, rising from the long grass of the meadow like mist, and scarcely stronger than that vapor—rather sorry specimens of their kind, too minor even to groan. Given enough time, of course, Arnogle could, with great effort and skill, call up a dozen or so middling-powerful specters, but such summoning wasn't Arnogle's strength. That was why he had tracked down the teenaged boy who was making his village a virtual ghost town. Arnogle had sent one of his own peasants to trade with the villagers, making sure to mention what a kind lord his master was and how willing to teach his art. Sure enough, Blaize had found a way to escape from his lord and flee to Arnogle, who had generously enlisted him as apprentice, thereby winning the eternal gratitude of both the boy, who escaped his neighbors' wrath and censure, and of the villagers, who breathed a massive sigh of relief at being rid of all the specters Blaize attracted. Arnogle had taught Blaize quickly enough how to control his ability to call the ghosts.

He used it now, surreptitiously adding his own calling to Arnogle's—and sure enough, it wasn't necessary to spread his arms. The ghosts rose from the trees at the edges of the meadow, boiled forth from the stream, even materialized from the air itself. Scores of them flocked toward Arnogle with long, drawn-out moans.

"Thank you, boy," Arnogle called, then bent to the silent task of cajoling the spirits, mind to mind, into helping him fight his enemy Pilochin.

Blaize watched in admiration. He could scarcely talk to the ghosts he summoned—that he could do so at all was a testament to Arnogle's teaching. Given a few more years of work under the master's expert guidance, he would probably be able to bargain with the ghosts well enough to achieve his ends, for Arnogle was as skilled a teacher as he was a ghost-leader.

If he survived! There, at the far side of the meadow, Pilochin came forth with a dozen men-at-arms and five apprentices, bearing the tank, hose, and nozzle of his magic. For a moment, Blaize entertained his old skeptical doubt that fire-casting was actually magical at all, but only a very clever use of devices and potions; its secrets were certainly well guarded. But he shoved the thought away—mechanics or magic, it could certainly slay himself and Arnogle this night, and every one of Arnogle's dozen guards to boot. Besides, Blaize couldn't deny that Pilochin knew all the minor spells for love philters, drying up cows' udders, disease curses, and all the other day-to-day magics that were necessary for any magician to keep his peasants in order—and bent to his will.

Blaize understood that the peasants were going to have a

master, no matter what, and if it weren't a kind and just master, it would be a tyrant—so he had determined to become a magician in order to oust the despot who ruled his home village and made his parents' lives miserable. Then Blaize would become lord himself—and would be a kind master.

Tonight, though, he might be without a master himself. He knew that ghost-leaders didn't usually fare too well against fire-hurlers. When all was said and done, specters might be frightening, but fire was lethal.

Arnogle must have finished, for the ghosts turned, howling like furies, and sped off toward Pilochin's men. The apprentices around the tank held their ground until the wraiths were almost upon them. Then one or two stepped back, then another—then all five were running pell-mell away, leaving Pilochin to saw the air with his arms, shouting in a rage at the ghosts, as though any of his spells could have stopped them. No, past him they went, chasing his men. Pilochin turned to glare at his rival, but Arnogle gave a shout of triumph. "Upon him, my men! Bring him home bound and trussed!"

The guards cheered and charged toward the lone magician. Pilochin stood rigid with defiance, then wavered, then finally turned to run.

With a hoot of delight, Arnogle ran to take possession of the firetank, shouting, "Come on, boy! Spoils to the victor!"

But Blaize stood a moment irresolute; it had all been too easy, far too easy. Both wizards brought only bodyguards, because more men could not be trusted. What use were armies when this issue would be decided by magic? Pilochin's levies would have run in fright from the ghosts, and his sheets of flame would have stampeded Arnogle's plowboys. Better by far to bring only the veterans of his bodyguard, who could be relied on to hold their places no matter how frightful the assault.

But Pilochin's bodyguards had fled like the greenest recruits when any seasoned soldier would have stood his ground, knowing the ghosts could do little but frighten. Oh, they could tell tales so gruesome as to make the most hardened murderer quake inside—but nothing more. They could send tendrils of madness into a man's mind, make him turn his weapons on those beside him, but they themselves could do little with their own hands, and any troops used to their assaults could withstand them.

Then why had Pilochin's men fled?

Arnogle seized the firetank with a cry of victory—a tank to which the hose was not even connected, and suddenly Blaize realized the trap. He cried out, "No, Teacher! They would not let their mystery fall into our hands, they would not—"

But Arnogle's bodyguards clustered around to help him with the waist-high tank. All together, they laid hold of the ring at its top, then lifted, and some premonition of disaster made Blaize throw himself on the ground a split second before the tank burst into a huge yellow ball of flame, devouring Arnogle and his bodyguards with a ravening roar. A wave of heat washed over Blaize; he hugged the ground, eyes shut tight, until cool air followed hot. Then he dared look up to see Pilochin pointing at him and crying, "There! Seize his apprentice! Then on to make sure of his lands and serfs!"

The guards came running back, and Blaize scrambled to his feet, turning to run, tearing off the robe that tangled his legs as he ran stumbling and staggering over the rough ground, blinking away hot tears that threatened to press out from his eyes, tears for Arnogle and for his valiant guards.

As he ran, Blaize called out, "Aid me, those who have answered my call! Protect me from those who chase me, I beg of you!"

His mind went where his voice did. Most of the ghosts ignored it, but a few understood his predicament and swooped at Pilochin and his apprentices, moaning and howling with distress and warning—but not enough; Pilochin's guards dodged and ran around the spirits, who swerved to follow, misty arms reaching out to seize, brows lowering over hollow eyes in anger. The guards ducked beneath them, though; one or two even ran right through a ghost. They came out shuddering with cold but ran all the faster for it.

Nonetheless, the swerving and dodging slowed them badly—slowed them enough so that Blaize was able to plunge into the cover of the woods. His ghostly friends had bought him just enough time.

There was no light as he fled, and soon a low limb knocked off the tall cone of his apprentice-magician's hat. A small ghost sailed before him, though, its glow just enough to let him see roots and fallen branches in his path. Even so, he stumbled now and again, but he plowed ahead with determination, certainly running faster than Pilochin's men, who had no guide and had to thrash about in strange territory. Blaize could hear their cursing, but it grew fainter with every passing minute. He risked a glance backward and saw a dozen dots of light bobbing and weaving. They had brought lanterns, then, but the flames couldn't possibly cast enough light for them to see the trail very far ahead. Even as he watched, one lantern dipped suddenly, shooting to the ground, and Blaize heard the cursing of a man who had tripped.

The ghost moaned in warning and Blaize turned back to his own trail just in time to see and leap a huge bulging root. He leaped it and followed his spectral guide, who zigged and zagged so often that in a matter of minutes Blaize was sure he had lost his pursuers. Still the ghost sailed onward until at last it stopped, turning back to Blaize with a groan that soared into a laugh of delight, and Blaize could make out the very faint thought, in the back of his mind, that he was safe now. He sent a rush of thanks outward to the ghost, who winked before disappearing.

Alone at last, Blaize sank to his knees, gasping for breath. Still, alarm pushed him, and he stood up again as soon as he could, no longer panting, but sorely weakened. He decided to turn toward the southwest and his home village—after all, Pilochin probably had no idea where Blaize had grown up.

Then he stopped, wide-eyed and apprehensive, looking at the trees about him, and realizing that it wasn't only Pilochin's men he had lost, but himself, too.

2

W hat does he mean, no *recorded* planet?" Alea asked.

"Just what you're thinking." Magnus grinned. "And so am I. Which of us thought it first?"

"Both at the same time." Alea spoke sharply to hide the hope that she might be a more talented telepath than she knew. "There is such a thing as coincidence, you know."

"Yes, and similar answers to the same question," Magnus said. "But we both think it's a lost colony, so let's see if we're right. Vision, Herkimer, please."

The image that appeared was flat, an elongated rectangle in bright colors. "Rather primitive," Herkimer explained. "The picture was originally displayed on a screen."

"Yes, we understand that it was television, not holovision— but this was a colony, after all, and bound to lack a few of the refinements." Magnus's gaze was glued to the picture before them.

They saw a man with long black hair and beard, wearing a burgundy robe, standing in front of a scene showing people in leather jerkins and hose with hawks on their forearms and shoulders. He was saying, ". . . steady progress in terraforming and developing the land. The Dragon Clan has perfected the taming and training of the local wyverns. Watch, now, as the dragoneer sends the beast hunting."

One of the leather-clad men swelled in the picture, and Alea saw that the reddish-brown creature on his wrist was no bird, but a sort of pterodactyl, though its head did look rather like that of a horse and its neck and backbone sprouted a row of triangular plates that stretched down its tail to an arrowpoint on the end. Now she realized why its handler wore leather—the claws were long, hooked, and sharp.

The man tossed his wrist and the wyvern leaped into the air, wings beating until it found an updraft. The picture stayed with it, following, making it larger and larger in the screen as it spiraled upward, riding the wind, then suddenly plummeted to earth. It rose again in an instant with a small animal in its claws—but grew smaller and smaller in the picture; its handler and his friends appeared at the edge and zoomed toward the middle, and the narrator swam back in front of them. He watched them, nodding, as the wyvern settled back onto its handler's wrist. "The dragoneer tells us the secret to controlling the reptile is thinking with it, every step of the way. Whether by mind reading or by training, the little dragons are bringing home dinner for their handlers as well as themselves."

He turned to smile at his viewers as the picture behind him dissolved into a scene of a broad wheat field. "Halfway across the continent, the Clan of the Mantis has succeeded in breeding insect predators that banished the crop feeders destroying their wheat."

The wheat behind him expanded until a few huge heads of grain filled the screen. Alea found herself looking at a dozen beetles stripping the grain from the stalk astonishingly quickly, but a bigger beetle came crawling behind them to gobble them up like so many pieces of candy.

"Neatly and efficiently done," the narrator said cheerfully. "In this case, big bugs have little bugs for biting."

He went on, the picture changing behind him as he told all the latest tidbits with delight. The Khayyam Clan had perfected its geodesic tent; a few people stood near the structure to show that it was three times their height. The Polite Barbarian Clan had plotted the grasslands available to each of the cattle-herding clans during each season. The Appleseed Clan was sending couriers to all the other clans with seeds for their new insect-resistant varieties of fruit.

Magnus sat, dazed by the variety of clans and the way in which they had split up the task of developing the planet. "Truly amazing," he murmured.

"But how long has it been? Several hundred years at least." Alea frowned. "And they're still adapting themselves to their world?" Then she answered her own question. "No, of course not. These pictures are coming to us at the speed of light, radiating outward from the planet, and the oldest ones reach us first."

Magnus gazed at her, feeling himself swell with pride, even though it was Herkimer who was her teacher, not himself. But she learned so quickly and reasoned out so much from it! Really, it was an honor to be her companion.

The narrator before them went on as the scene displayed a picture of a dozen saffron-robed people, the men bearded, the women without cosmetics and with simple hairstyles. Most had gray hair; all looked compassionate and concerned. The narrator told his viewers, "The gurus of all the clans tell us that their people are paying entirely too much attention to worldly things."

Behind him, the picture changed to a grid with the faces of

men and women in small squares. Most of them were gray-haired, too, but they fairly glowed with enthusiasm.

"The clan leaders held a teleconference to consider that issue," the narrator told his viewers, "and replied that all the clans together were performing a massive study in ecology, though that may not have been what they intended. By developing their animals and crops, they're gaining a greater sense of how all life-forms fit together and interact. The clan leaders claim this is another route toward achieving harmony with the Infinite—and the gurus agreed! I do have to say, though, that the Wise Ones didn't seem too enthusiastic about it."

Alea objected, "The people in each of those 'clans' don't look anything like one another! How could they be related?"

"They probably aren't," Gar replied, "or at least they weren't, until their mothers and fathers married. I suspect they share interests, not genes. People concerned with herding cattle band together, people who want to grow oats band together, and those who want to raise maize gather together, too."

"Well, that makes sense," Alea admitted. "After all, oats and maize grow best in different climates—and their farmers would have to live together."

"Besides, village life that way would give them the feeling of belonging to an extended family," Gar said thoughtfully, "and I suspect these colonists were very lonely before they formed a group."

The narrator's voice began to crackle and the picture broke up into a swirling mass of colored dots.

Alea frowned. "What's happening? Oh! We're going toward the planet faster than light."

"Correct, Alea," Herkimer's voice said. "We have passed the range of the oldest television signal emitted from the planet. There are younger ones, of course. How many years should I let pass by us before I record one to display again?"

"Let pass?" Alea frowned. "How many are there?"

"An uninterrupted stream, broadcasting over a period of a hundred years or more."

"Only one century?" Magnus's eyes glittered. "There should be seven. Let's see what happened." He turned to Alea. "Every twenty-five years?"

"That should give us some idea of their progress," Alea agreed—but she felt misgivings, felt out of her depth, so she asked, "Why so many?"

"I want a quick overview of the planet," Gar explained.

"But we gain it by moving closer to the planet," Alea objected. "If we decide we want more detail, it will be too late to go back and find it."

She expected him to argue and felt her blood quicken with the thought, but Magnus only nodded judiciously and said, "A good idea. Store all the signals, Herkimer, but show us only those that come in every quarter-century. Then if we wish to retrieve others, we can."

Alea felt both pleased and chagrined: pleased that he took her thoughts seriously, chagrined that she had missed a chance for an argument. Magnus knew how to argue properly—taking her seriously and intending to win, but not too seriously and not minding if she proved to be right.

For the next hour, Herkimer showed them snippets of dramas, comedies, programs of singers and dancers, and shows in which ordinary people matched wits against a master of ceremonies—though they called him a guru—trying to answer obscure questions such as, "When was the *I Ching* written?"

Alea stared in blank incomprehension. "Is there any point to these pantomimes?"

"I'm sure the people who watched them thought so." Magnus's brow was creased in thought. "What I find interesting is the people's appearance, and the subjects that seem to interest them."

"They all wear such primitive clothing!" said Alea.

"Everyone does seem to wear a robe, unless they're working," Magnus agreed. "But their working gear isn't all that different from your own people's."

Alea shrugged. "Didn't you tell me that tunics and leggins are timeless?"

"Yes, until the leggins turn into trousers. Strange that there should be so many ghost stories, though."

"Yes." Alea smiled. "The ghosts seem to have more amusing remarks than the live people. And they do like stories about magic, don't they?"

"Yes, but I wish we'd seen more of that documentary about wyverns. They seem to be very interesting beasts. I'm amazed that they managed to survive the introduction of the birds the colonists brought with them."

"Why?" Alea turned to him with a frown. "With those beaks and claws, even an eagle would flee them."

"Pterodactyls didn't fare so well against birds on old Earth," Magnus explained, "though that may have been due to the cold snap that killed off most of the dinosaurs."

"Yes, dragons by any other name. I haven't seen any sign of them on these programs."

"Something must have killed them off, then—the wyverns didn't evolve in a vacuum."

"Wait—what's this?" Alea leaned forward, frowning.

The picture was rough, grainy, and flashed lines of static now and then—a gaunt woman in a rough tunic pointing to pictures on an easel, which abruptly filled the screen as she explained them. "Native plants have begun to grow again, now that the Maize Clan has run out of weed-killers from Terra . . . the Grape Clan sends word that their new vines are only root stock, so that the hybrid vines brought from Terra are the last of the stronger grapes that we'll see. Without new seeds and shoots from the home planet, they're having to make do with the weaker strains that are offspring of the old vines, and the native weeds are choking many of them. People are stockpiling the old vintages. The Equestrian Clan reports that without imported sperm and ova, many foals are dying from local diseases, but the survivors are developing hybrid colts and fillies that are more hardy, though not as tall or graceful. The Aurochs Clan is sending in a similar report—their new cattle are smaller and stronger, though with much less meat—but all the livestock clans are producing plenty of fertilizer. Unfortunately, it doesn't seem to be bonding with the soil as well as the Terran fertilizers did, and the yield per acre is down considerably."

She looked up at the camera, drawn and haggard. "Fortunately we have enough food stocks for the next five years, and the Alchemist Clan reports great success in developing philters that remove the toxins from native plants." She turned to pull a picture of strange, broad-leaved plants off the easel, revealing a picture of a misty humanoid form floating between two thatched roofs. "The Ghost Clan has confirmed yesterday's report of a new haunting in the Amity Valley. They haven't, however, confirmed Goren Hafvie's claim that the spirit is the ghost of his ancestor, Guru Plenvie."

"They can't believe ghosts are real!" Alea exclaimed.

"It's a belief that never seems to die out, even in technologically advanced societies." Magnus carefully didn't remind her that she herself had believed in ghosts only two years before.

"In the northeast, the druids of the Quarry Clan have expelled a group of thirteen men and women for trying to intimidate the rest of their village by threats of spreading a disease called murrain among their cattle," the narrator went on. The picture on the easel slid away to expose a scene of four cows and a bull lying on their sides, swollen as though inflated. "Unfortunately, an epidemic did spread through the village's livestock. The druids examined the bodies and concluded that the cause really was magic. They expelled the sorcerers with a warning to establish their own village and stay away from any others." The narrator filled the screen again, the picture suddenly small behind her. "Since Terra has cut us off and is no longer sending cattle embryos, spreading such a disease has become a serious crime."

The picture broke into colored dots, the voice was drowned in a rush of static, and Alea stared, feeling numbed. "So that's what happened to the colony planets when Terra cut them off?"

"To all of them, yes." Magnus nodded. "Some were more self-sufficient than others, but in most, the PEST regime's retrenchment meant famine and plague—and war, as the people fought over what food stocks remained." His face was gaunt, haunted. "I hope we won't have to watch such a bloodbath here."

"It seems we will." Alea braced herself as the picture reformed in front of them, showing two men in half-armor and high boots, halberds in hand, pushing two raggedly dressed men into a small mud hut lit only by a tiny fire in the center.

"You can't leave us here, Corporal!" one of the ragged men whined. "We'll starve, that's what!"

"Do what you please," one of the soldiers grunted. "Anybody who steals from the soldiers' mess deserves what he gets!"

"You can say that again." The other man sniffed with disdain. "Lumpy porridge and stale hardtack—no wonder they call it a mess!"

The other soldier swung a punch at him; the man adroitly ducked. "You liked it well enough to try to steal a bowlful when you were supposed to be peeling potatoes," the guard growled.

"You can just wait here until the company magus has time for you!"

"The company magus!" The first man shuddered. "You hear that, Charlie? He'll give us lockjaw so bad we can't even sip!"

"The punishment will fit the crime," the soldier threatened.

"You don't mean he's going to throw us into fits for punishment!" Charlie bleated.

"I could think of someplace better to throw you," the guard growled. "Shut up, now, and wait your turn."

"A tern wouldn't be half-bad roasted," Charlie mused. "The wings are kind of bony, though."

"I thought they made a jingling noise," the first rag man said, and turned to the guard. "Can we wing for service?"

Alea stared, unbelieving. "They're joking!"

"If you can call those jokes," Magnus groaned. "I don't think we have to worry about seeing a war—they're still making comedy programs."

"Pretty poor program," Alea said, "with only a mud hut for a scene."

"Pretty poor comedy," Magnus replied.

"I'll show you service!" The guard yanked a length of rope from his waist. "Pozzo, go get a bowl of mush."

The other guard grinned and went out the door.

The first guard tied the rope through the bonds on Charlie's wrists, then passed it through a ring set in the wall and tied the other end to George's wrists. The other guard came back in with a steaming bowl of porridge and set it just a little too far away for the two thieves to reach. Both soldiers went out, grinning and laughing, and for the next ten minutes, Alea and Magnus watched the two men's antics as they tried to reach the bowl of porridge. First they both lunged at it and were brought up short, their hands jerking up higher behind their backs. Alea winced with the thought of their pain, but the two men seemed far more distressed at not being able to reach the bowl. Then Charlie stood up and held his wrists right next to the ring on the wall while George hobbled forward on his knees, leaning as far as he could—but the bowl was still out of reach. Chagrined, he stood up and retreated, letting Charlie try, and Charlie did manage to step through his bound wrists, bringing them in front of him—but that kept him even farther from the bowl, so he stepped back through, but was no better able to reach the bowl than George had been. Then the two tried to untie each other's wrists with their teeth, giving them scope for many ribald comments. At last George sat down and reached with his feet, trying to pull the bowl toward him. Charlie realized what he was doing and stepped through his wrists again, then held them next to the iron ring, and George squirmed forward, wrapping his feet around the bowl and pulling it in, but just as he was about to sink his face into the mush, the guard came in to untie them, informing them that the magician was ready for them. The two men stumbled out of the hut with howls of dismay. A disembodied voice told Alea and Magnus, "See what happens to Charlie and George next week, when . . ." before his voice was drowned in static and the picture turned into another sea of colored dots.

Alea sat, numbed and amazed. "They're making fun of it! They're actually making fun of war! Or of army life, at least." '

"It can't be so bad a fight as all that," Magnus said. "Either a very small war, or a very short one."

"Perhaps," Alea said, "but there must have been some kind of war, or there wouldn't be soldiers arresting them!"

"And famine," Magnus agreed, "or they wouldn't be trying to steal a bowl of porridge—and punished for it. But if they could laugh at it so quickly, it must have been short."

"Now, wait," Alea protested. "This was twenty-five years after that last news program, wasn't it?"

"No," Herkimer said. "Only ten years. I thought you might find it interesting."

"We certainly did," Alea said, still feeling numb. "What else were these people watching?"

Herkimer showed them snippets of very crudely made dramas and comedies; the subject matter alternated between war and famine on the one hand, and magic and astrology on the other. Pagan gods frequently meddled with the people, confusing the issues tremendously—and sometimes resolving them.

"What kind of civilization is this," Magnus asked, "where war mixes with magic and mysticism?"

Alea smiled thinly. "It sounds like my own people."

"Let us hope their war is past!" Magnus said fervently. "How many years have we skipped through, Herkimer?"

"A hundred seventy-eight, Magnus. The quality of the signal has been deteriorating steadily. I am having to process it more and more elaborately in order to present a coherent picture."

"Thanks for your efforts," Magnus said. "Let's see the next program."

The screen appeared again, showing a worn and haggard woman sitting at a desk in a harsh and glaring light with stark shadows. On the desk stood an easel holding pictures. As she finished one story she pulled the picture from the easel, revealing another. The camera moved closer to fill the screen with the easel picture, wobbling as it went, then moved back out to include the woman again.

"Remember, these pictures are several weeks old," she told her audience. "They've been sent to us by post riders, since our ancestors' gadgets won't send pictures by wire anymore. To be blunt, they don't work."

Magnus darted a dismayed glance at Alea; she met it with consternation of her own.

The woman started talking again, drawing their gazes back to her. "Plague has broken out in Oldmarket City, Ebor City, Holborn City, and Exbury Big Town. Their people are fleeing into the countryside. They may carry plague germs with them. Avoid strangers. It will prove impossible to keep them out of your towns—there are just too many of them—so I recommend evacuation. Take your valuables and your treasured mementos and go live in the forest—city people like me are afraid of the woods and the wild animals. Let them have your towns; keep your lives."

"I wouldn't take her advice for a second!" Alea said. "I would think she was just trying to frighten me away so somebody could steal my house!"

"Then the villagers probably thought that, too," Magnus said, troubled. "I wonder how badly they fought over a handful of cottages?"

"The other cities have no disease yet," the woman told them, "but farmers are afraid to bring them grain and other foodstuffs, so prices have skyrocketed and bread riots have broken out here and there. Gurus and magicians have managed to quiet them. Still, if you are a farmer watching this broadcast, please take your extra harvest to the city nearest you; you'll receive at least ten times the usual price."

"Who does she think she's fooling?" Alea demanded. "If the farmers know about germs, they know that people from one city visit other cities every day. They may get a high price, but they'll bring home plague as well as money!"

"I'm afraid the farmers did realize that," Magnus said sadly. "I wonder how long it took before the city people came out to the countryside as a mob, to take whatever food they could find?"

Alea shuddered. "Then the plague probably swept the whole continent!"

"Here in Lutabor, the power plant has stopped working," the woman said. "We're only able to stay on the air because we have our own generator, but we don't know how much longer our fuel will last, and the methane plants have stopped operating. The weather's getting colder, so people are moving out to the countryside where they can at least keep themselves warm by burning fallen trees."

"And steal farmers' houses," Alea whispered, staring in dismay.

"The fighting must have been desperate," Magnus agreed.

"It's the end of a world!" Alea breathed.

"And the beginning of a new one." Magnus frowned. "Assuming they didn't all die out. I wonder what we'll find there."

"We'll have to end this broadcast now," the woman said. "We'll talk to you again tomorrow if we can. Remember, please, if you live in any of the small towns around Lutabor—our refugees have no disease, but they do have money for buying food, so there's no need to be afraid of any of us. That's all we can manage today. We wish you well, and I hope I'll be able to talk to you again."

"Was she?" Alea asked as static replaced the picture.

3

*'m afraid not," Herkimer said. "That was the last television broadcast from the planet. There are still radio broadcasts coming in, but the signals are of very low quality and the announcing amateurish. Their news programs are clearly rumor and devoted to superstitious nonsense, such as communicating with the dead, magic, and hauntings."

Alea looked skeptical at the word "superstitious," but Magnus said, "They described a civilization falling apart."

"It would seem so," Herkimer agreed. "We will be close enough to commence orbit in twenty-six hours. Perhaps a photographic survey will clarify matters somewhat."

It did, but not for the better. The pictures Herkimer presented them showed magnificent cities that, on closer inspection, featured broken windows, tumbled masonry, and streets choked with rubble, empty except for small bands of people, some deformed. Here and there, the pictures showed pitched battles.

"The cities certainly died," Magnus said, his face tragic.

"There seem to be a few who couldn't bear to leave." Suddenly Alea stiffened. "Magnify, Herkimer!"

The band in the center of the screen jumped outward to fill it. There were five people—two men and a woman wearing patched tunics and coarse leggins, and two others who wore hooded robes. One of the men walked hunched over by a bent spine, another limped with a twisted foot. The woman glanced up at the sky to gauge the weather, and they saw she had only one eye, the other covered by a patch.

"Nobody wanted them around," Alea whispered.

"So the cities are sanctuaries for the outcasts," Magnus said, his face grave. "Let's have a look at the countryside, Herkimer."

The city street dissolved into an expanse of patchwork fields dotted by small villages with thatched roofs—but as the landscape unrolled below them, they saw larger towns clustered around central hills upon which stood mansions in front of broad courtyards surrounded by smaller buildings.

"No castles, at least." Magnus frowned. "It's not quite a feudal setup."

"Isn't it?" Alea asked. "Could we have a closer look at one of those mansions, Herkimer?"

"Of course," the computer answered, and one huge house swam toward them until it filled the screen.

"It's made of stone," Alea pointed out, "and the walls are pretty thick, to judge by the depth of the windows—which aren't all that large, by the way."

"No, they're not," Magnus agreed. "Three feet high at the most, and maybe two wide. Not a fortress, but it would still be hard to capture."

"There are no walls around the property, though," Alea admitted, "so they can't be too worried about attack. Either that, or their weapons are so powerful that the walls would only be there for privacy."

"Let's hope it just means a peaceful culture," Magnus said.

"But one with rulers and subjects," Alea pointed out. "See how many people are out there working in the fields?"

"That could simply mean that everyone works." Then Magnus saw the woman in green silk riding on a gray horse and the man in velvet and brocade who rode the chestnut stallion beside her, with several liveried guards behind them. "Or it could mean a rigid class system."

"You *would* raise a question." Alea glanced at him with annoyance. "Now I want to go down there just to find out the answer."

"So do I," Magnus admitted. "Even more, though, I want to find out why they're so sure of the peace. No one's wearing armor, and that isn't a very large troop of bodyguards." He added as an afterthought, "Of course, the peasants *could* be oppressed."

Alea shrugged. "How badly? We've seen worse, much worse. Besides, you can't tell just by looking at them."

"Yes, though Brigante was the first planet I've seen where that wasn't true."

Alea shrugged. "All we could see from orbit was that there was a priestly class and a peasant class. It made sense that the priests should have been exploiting the peasants."

"Yes, and it took a dirtside tour to find out that the people were really quite happy." Magnus winced at the memory of a civilization that had no government above the level of a town council—if you didn't count the secret society that had virtually become the government.

Evanescent's telepathic species had a great deal to do with the smooth running of Brigante's society, too, and was where the alien had joined them—though only Alea knew about her, and at the moment, even she didn't remember.

"Displaying catalog," Herkimer said, and the screen before

them became a collection of small pictures arranged in three walls, one behind the other.

Magnus glanced from one frame to another. "A medieval civilization amid the ruins of a modern one—well, I've seen that before."

Alea thought of her home world and winced. "We'll have to be on the watch for people who remember how to use the old machines—or even to build new ones." She remembered the dwarves of Midgard building radio transceivers.

"Well, we won't learn anything more up here." Magnus stood up. "Cancel display, Herkimer, and fabricate us some costumes like the ones we've seen, would you?"

The picture-walls disappeared, and Herkimer asked, "Costumes of the privileged class or the peasantry, Magnus?"

"Do you feel like being a lady of wealth and breeding this time?" Magnus asked Alea.

"A peasant will be fine, thank you." Alea had a grudge against the wealthy and privileged. "Besides, the ruling class is so small that they probably all know each other and would be very suspicious of strangers."

"True," Magnus agreed. "Peasants, Herkimer. We'll start at the bottom and work our way up, as usual."

Alea stood, too. "Should I start calling you Gar Pike again?"

"That would be wise," Magnus said, nodding.

"I don't know why you bother with that alias," Alea grumbled. "No one here is going to know who Magnus d'Armand is."

"Only the wrong people."

"You mean SCENT agents. We don't even know that there *are* any of them working here."

"In fact, there probably aren't," Gar said, "but it's one chance we don't have to take. I'd prefer my former colleagues don't recognize me if they do happen to be in the neighborhood." The fact that SCENT was also his father's organization was just as much of a problem—the name "d'Armand" was rather famous among their ranks.

Privately, Alea suspected that Magnus would be easy to recognize under any name—on backward planets where nutrition was rarely what it should be, there weren't very many men who were nearly seven feet tall. On the other hand, there weren't many women who were six feet four inches, either. Even on her home world she had stood out, to her sorrow. She once again felt an overwhelming rush of gratitude to Magnus for taking her away from that misery, but stiffened her face, determined not to let it show.

Magnus misunderstood the expression; his voice lowered, becoming gentler. "Come now, it won't be all that bad. We'll probably discover that the peasants are well fed and well clothed, and quite happy with their lot. Besides, we could do with a touch of sun and fresh air again."

"And rain!" Alea's pulse quickened at the thought. Truth to tell, she would have taken shore leave even if nobody on the planet needed her—after six months shipboard, she was glad of an excuse to go outdoors again.

So was Evanescent, of course, but she didn't bother telling the humans—or even reminding them that she existed. There would be time enough for that, if it were necessary.

The next shipboard day, Herkimer spiraled around the planet Oldeira to the night side, where he settled into a clearing in a forest, not far from a road, that led to a village only a few miles away. Magnus and Alea went down the gangplank, he with a spring in his step, she nearly dancing. They picked their way across the clearing by the light of a lantern that had a very medieval look, then disappeared into the trees.

Herkimer remained, gangplank extended, though usually he would have lifted off as soon as they had disembarked and been halfway back to orbit before the humans had reached the forest. Now, though, the ship still sat, as though trying to re-member what it was supposed to do next—until Evanescent prowled down the gangplank, a huge ball of a cat face with a foreshortened feline body that seemed much too small. None-theless, she moved with fluidity and grace as she disappeared into the forest, following the trail of the humans' thoughts.

Only then did the gangplank slide back into the ship and Herkimer rise into the night sky, not even knowing that his computer-brain had been dormant for a few minutes. He wouldn't even think to compare his memories to the ship's clock, for how could he have lost time without being aware of it?

They broke out of the underbrush onto the road. Alea looked up at the narrow strip of sky, so strewn with stars that it gave as much light as a full moon on Terra. Then she turned to Gar. "What do we do now? Look for a guide?"

"I usually do," Gar admitted, "preferably someone who's planning to keep traveling for a while."

"Meaning someone on the run," Alea interpreted, "who has no love for the local government but needs protection."

"Yes," Gar said, "but not a real criminal, just a good person who's fallen into trouble—a soldier on the losing side, perhaps, or a peasant who couldn't pay his taxes."

"That shouldn't be hard to find, in a medieval society." Alea turned to face the road. "Let's just hope we find them before the real outlaws do."

Mira had managed to stay free for two days—nights, rather, since she didn't dare travel when it was light and the soldiers could see her. She had hidden in a haystack the first day and watched between the straws as a party of them rode by. They hadn't brought the dogs then, thank heaven, or she would have been discovered. The second night, she had waded down a stream until her feet were numb, then managed to climb a vine to a tree limb, where she had warmed her feet until she was sure of them again, and could walk the lower limbs from tree to tree until they were too far apart to cross from one to another. By that time, though, she had been at least a hundred feet from the bank, and the hounds weren't likely to pick up her scent if they'd been following the water.

There were dangers at night, of course, and she went with her heart pounding, starting at every noise, frightened at the mere thought of the ghosts who were apt to come looking for her—but the magician hadn't sent them yet. Wild ghosts were even more frightening, for she'd heard stories about them taking over people's minds—though just as many stories claimed that couldn't happen till a person was dead, and then it would be ghost against ghost, and surely the newer would be stronger and would win.

This was the third night, and she doubted that the hounds and the soldiers would hunt her so far from home, so she dared to walk on the road instead of picking her way over tree roots under the shadows of the pines. Roketh would send word to the other magicians, though, and their guards would be alert for a woman traveling alone. If they found her, they would chase her, catch her, and send her back to Roketh—so she still went cautiously, alert for the sound of hooves or marching feet. She was just beginning to breathe more easily when she saw the glimmering mist gathering over the road ahead of her. She stopped, heart in her throat, and watched, rooted to the spot, as the mist thickened and bulged into arms and a head with hollow, staring eyes and a dark circle of a mouth—but nothing more, only a blank bulge with darkness for features. It was raw energy, a specter gathered but still unformed, a wild ghost, a thing seeking form and purpose. Its kind were the most dangerous sort of phantoms, for they were voracious.

It shot toward her, moaning, and her heart leaped into her throat.

Gar was pouring the first ladle of stew into Alea's bowl when the terror hit; he nearly dropped both back into the kettle.

Alea's head snapped back as though she had been slapped. "Who was that?"

"I don't know, but I would hate to be the one they're threatening," Gar said grimly. "Whoever sent that mental bolt finds a great deal of pleasure in others' fright—and the woman whom it hit is absolutely terrified. If you'll excuse me, I have to see a sadist about a beating."

"I won't excuse you at all." Alea rose, catching up her staff. "First one to him gets to keep him." As an afterthought, she added, "Put that fire out, will you?"

Gar stared down at the flames; they diminished and died. The sticks smoked, but even the smoke thinned and vanished. Then Gar looked up to find that Alea had disappeared into the night.

The ghost's lament turned into words: "Erring woman, go back to your master!"

"No!" Mira wailed. "He will exploit me, he will abuse me, he will hurt me!"

"Shame!" the ghost intoned, towering over her. "Shame! Shame!"

"It is shame he would heap upon me!" Mira felt hot tears streaming down her cheeks. "I have seen the women he has used—empty husks, all the spirit drained from them." Then she broke off, staring in horror as she realized what had happened to those women—and why the ghosts were willing to help chase escaped women back to Roketh. "You want my spirit when he is done with me! He will drain me of life and energy and give them to you!"

"Go back!" the ghost moaned, reaching out to point with a gossamer finger. "Hear the cries of those who chase! Go back before they tear you, rend you!"

Then Mira heard it in the distance—the wild baying of monstrous hounds.

Alea's thoughts had been as easy to trace as tracks in snow, of course, not to mention the fact that she was running down a road; where else could she go? But Gar reasoned that the chase might be a long one, so he steadied into an easy lope that covered maximum distance with minimum energy. Even so, his longer legs began to catch up with Alea's. A glimmer in the road ahead alerted him—their quarry, perhaps? But the glimmer seemed to grow until he saw what it was and slammed to a halt, almost colliding with Alea, who stood even more still, stiff with the supernatural fear of her childhood. "Those . . . those can't be real ghosts, can they?"

Seven glowing shapes towered over one young woman who stared up at them, poised to flee but frozen by fear.

"Real ghosts? Ridiculous!" But Gar had to force the scoffing tone. "Whatever they are, though, they're putting out an awful lot of psionic energy. We've got to put a damper on it."

"Yes! They're scaring the life out of that poor girl!" Alea jolted out of her trance. "The life? You don't suppose—?"

"One of those ghosts doesn't have a face," Gar said grimly. "Maybe he's looking for one. Let's go."

"Wait." Alea raised a hand against his chest. "Listen—with your ears!"

They were both silent a minute. Then Gar said, "Hoofbeats."

"Change of plan," Alea said, "not that we had one. Let's go in low."

Panic seized Mira; she spun and ran from the ghost—and from the dogs far behind.

The ghost's moan rose, quavering to a shriek, and more specters burst from the ground, broke from the trees, condensed from the very air in answer. As one, they swooped toward her from every side, converging, herding. She screamed and whirled about, thinking to dare the first ghost alone instead of the six who swooped toward her, but the phantom had disappeared. Hope leaped as she plunged toward the clear space and the trees beyond.

The earth exploded into fire before her. She shrank back shrieking, whirling to run again, but the ghosts parted to let three horsemen ride through, one from each side, racing to be first upon her, hands reaching down to catch. With a soldier at either hand and the flames at her back, Mira shrank to her knees, whimpering, crying out against the injustice of so many against one woman.

A screech of anger ripped the night. Mira thought it was her own until a woman leaped in front of her, a woman unbelievably tall stepping in to swing her staff at the first of the riders. It caught him across the side of the head; he cried out as he fell. His two mates shouted and turned their horses, charging down at her, but as the one on the right plunged toward the woman, a huge dark shadow rose from the grass and swung an arm to catch the rider by the waist. The man gave a shout of anger, a shout quickly choked by the pressure on his belly; the horse galloped onward, jerking the stirrups off the man's feet. For a moment he kicked and flailed in the air; then the giant dropped him and he fell and lay, choking and trying to gasp, the wind knocked out of him.

Mira stared, unbelieving—partly at the size of the two strangers, partly at their skill, but mostly at the fact that they spun and kicked and struck in the midst of half a dozen keening ghosts without paying them the slightest attention.

The third rider bellowed a curse and swung a long club, but the woman's staff was longer and she jabbed it forward like a spear even as she sidestepped just enough for the horse to rush past her. The butt of the staff caught the man in the stomach; he shot off the rump of his horse, striking with his club as he did. It struck the woman's forearm, knocking down her staff, but the damage was done; "Have at you!" she spat as he scrambled to his feet, and swung the staff high one-handed, whirling it like a windmill.

The rider saw the power of that whirling weapon and stepped back, raising his club to guard.

The woman swung; he blocked, but the staff struck with ferocious momentum, knocking the club aside, then swinging high to strike again. The guard cried out in fear and leaped aside—but the giant came up behind him, catching his collar and yanking him off his feet. He struggled, kicking, and the giant spoke in a deep, mellow voice. "Not too hard, now. No need to murder."

"Do I need to strike at all?" The woman stepped up to glare at the guard, adroitly ducking his roundhouse punch. "Do I, cat's meat?"

"A murrain upon you!" the man snarled, and kicked.

The woman danced aside. "I take it that means 'yes.' " The staff swung and the man's eyes rolled up. The giant dropped him and heaved the burden he'd been dragging. Two more guards fell on top.

"Foully done!" the shapeless ghost intoned. "Fear, man, fear!"

"Fear?" The giant gazed off into space, seeming to examine something, then shook his head. "No, I don't think so."

"Fear, fool!" another ghost cried, one who bore the semblance of a hard-faced old woman in an antique gown. She thrust her fingers into the giant's head. "Shrivel in fright! Kneel in abject terr . . . aiiieeee!" She yanked her hands back; they glowed cherry-red. "He is a ghost-leader!"

"Unlike yourself, who is an ape-leader," the woman snapped.

"What is an ape?" one of the male ghosts demanded.

The female ghost turned and dived into the head of one of the horses. It was remarkable to see how her form diminished into a wedge, then narrowed even further as it sank in.

The horse's head snapped up, its eyes widening in terror then narrowing in rage. Its whinny was more a scream, high and wild, as it pivoted and thundered down on the giant.

4

The giant leaped aside, but not far enough; the horse's shoulder clipped him and he fell, tumbling head over heels.

"Gar!" the woman cried, and ran toward him, but three ghosts shot to bar her way, moaning in doleful harmony.

The possessed horse wheeled, rearing, iron-clad hooves poised to strike the giant as he strove to regain his feet.

The woman shied away from the ghosts in fright for a moment; then her lips thinned, and she charged right through the nearest.

She came out shivering but swinging her staff like a scythe, smacking into the back of the horse's hind leg. It folded; with a scream, the horse fell back. Even with one leg weakened, it turned to face this new antagonist, forelegs raised to strike, lips pulled back to show teeth that seemed to glow in the night.

The woman struck one foreleg. The horse screamed again and she pushed the butt into its mouth. It bit down in fury, but its eyes locked with hers. Her voice vibrated with a strange energy as she chanted,

I am young and vital, and therefrom stems my might.
But you are aged and faded,
Your strength long since benighted,
Being only power stolen
From those you have affrighted.
Yield to me, hag I've fighted!
Get you hence from this poor beast!
Get you gone, and leave in peace!

The horse glared at her, eyes locked with hers, malevolence burning, but the giant came up, standing behind the woman and glaring as she did. The other ghosts swooped and shrieked and gibbered at them, but the two ignored them, locking eyes with the horse until it peeled back its teeth, opened its mouth wide in a shriek—and the hag's ghost shot forth from its mouth, taking the shriek with her, swelling to tower over them, howling in pain and fury even as the rage faded from the horse's eyes.

"Only what you deserve!" Alea spat at the old woman's shade. "Be still, or we'll do worse."

The ghost's scream cut off. "She's as bad as the mad folk in the cities!" she cried, staring at Alea in fright.

"Worse?" a man's ghost blustered. "What could you do worse?" But his tone was hollow with hidden dread.

"You don't want to know." The tall woman turned back to the horse, which blinked, confused, looked about itself in surprise, then struggled to rise and sank back on the injured leg with a doleful neigh.

The giant stepped up behind it to lay a hand on its head. It whipped its nose about to bite, but froze and calmed strangely. After a minute or two, it relaxed, folded its legs, and watched the proceedings with mild interest.

The tall woman turned to find Mira beset. Three ghosts towered over her, their moans growing louder and louder in a dissonance that grated on Mira's nerves; she clapped her hands over her ears. The tall woman winced but said, "Do I have to teach you to sing? Begone, fools, for even I can cause you pain!"

One of the ghosts—the one in the form of a guardsman in ancient livery with a long ragged scar that showed how he had died—clapped his hands to his head and shrieked. The other two stared at him in shock, then disappeared so suddenly they might never have been.

"Begone," the woman commanded the ghost-guard, and narrowed her eyes. His shriek soared higher; abruptly, he winked out.

"This cannot be!" the ghost of an old man quavered. His translucent robes shook with his trembling. "Mortals can only lead, persuade—they cannot command, for they cannot coerce!"

" 'Coerce' might be too strong a word," the giant admitted. "We can, however, cause you pain."

The ghost doubled over screaming as though stabbed in the belly.

"Begone!" the woman commanded.

The old man winked out. The last two ghosts drifted backward warily.

"What's a ghost without fetters?" the woman asked.

"An unchained malady," the giant answered, and glowing links appeared in midair with manacles at either end.

With a wail, the last two ghosts disappeared.

Mira knelt, trembling and wide-eyed. She flinched away as the woman came to her—but the stranger knelt, saying, "Don't fear, my dear, they won't harm you anymore, and neither shall we. We simply can't stand to see one against ten, no, especially not when three of them are armed and mounted, and the one is a woman alone." She caught Mira's hands in her own. "There now, the danger's past, and neither my Gar nor myself will offer you the slightest threat. You're safe with us."

"But—but . . ." Mira forced herself not to pull away but was so frightened of the power these two had shown, of their size and strength, that she was afraid to let herself believe, afraid to trust.

"Are we so intimidating, then?" the woman asked with a sad smile. "We shouldn't be, not to a poor lass alone in the night with bullies and ghosts out to chase her. Come, my name is Alea, and my companion is Gar. We both know what it is to flee and be chased, as you do, and would never dream of hurting one who has suffered as we have."

Mira wavered, wanting so badly to trust but not daring to— but Alea let go of Mira's hands and opened her arms. Yearning overcame fear, and Mira let herself fall into the other woman's embrace, sobbing as though her heart would break.

Alea simply held her and let her weep, now and again making soothing noises. Finally the storm passed and Mira leaned back and away a little, dashing the tears from her eyes. Over Alea's shoulder she could see the giant tying the unconscious riders over the horses' backs and shooing them away. Then he turned to frown at the wall of fire. Slowly the flames died, and the night was still.

Mira began to tremble again. "You are a magician." She turned to Alea, wide-eyed. "Both of you!"

"If this is what passes for a magician in this land, I suppose we are." The woman spoke angrily. "How foul is the man who would use such power to terrify a poor helpless girl! Tell us his name, damsel, so we will know him for a villain if we should be so unlucky as to meet him!"

"He—he is the lord of our village and fifty more like it, with all their acres." She clasped Alea's hands between her own. "But, oh, good people, I beg you not to go near him! Roketh is a magician of fearful power—a ghost-leader and fire-hurler both! He can persuade any ghost to do his bidding, even a wild almost-ghost who has no form yet hungers for a human spirit to devour so it can steal its shape! None can threaten him and live! He has slain six other magicians in combat and swallowed their lands and people!"

"Then perhaps he should disgorge them," Gar said heavily, coming to sit cross-legged near them.

"You must not attempt it! He would slay you!" Mira looked wide-eyed from the woman to the man and back, tense with fright at the thought. "None can stand against Roketh!"

"He may not be quite so invincible as he seems," Alea told her, "but we would certainly be fools if we rushed in to confront him without learning a great deal more about him. Don't worry, lass, we won't attack him out of hand. If nothing else, we must stay a while to travel with you and make sure you come to no harm."

"But Roketh will send soldiers after you! He will send ghosts, he will send apprentice magicians to hurl fire!"

"Why then, we must make sure they can't find us," Gar said easily.

Mira stared from one to the other as though they were crazed. "I hid my trail from the dogs, but the hunting-ghosts found me. How can you hide your mind from the specters?"

"So they follow your thoughts, do they?" Alea asked. "Don't worry, then, lass—we can shield our thoughts quite well, and yours, too." She glanced up at Gar. "Isn't that true?"

"Very," Gar confirmed. "More to the point, now that we know what they are, we should be able to tell when they're coming."

Mira thought of evading the ghosts and the despair of utter weariness overwhelmed her; she crumpled to the ground.

"What use is it to hide or flee? If Roketh does not find me again, some other magician will, and will claim me for his own for the same use Roketh intended, for there is no patch of ground in all this land that isn't the demesne of one magician or another!"

"Well, then, we must keep moving," Alea said with great practicality. "On the road or off it, we must keep marching until we find a place the magicians can't reach."

"There is no such place!"

"Then we'll have to make one," Gar said matter-of-factly.

Mira stared from one to the other. "You must be powerful magicians indeed, to speak so lightly of building what cannot be made!"

"We don't really think of it as magic," Gar protested.

Alea gave him a withering glance. "Speak for yourself, long thinker." She turned back to Mira. "Magic or not, he'll make it work. You'll be safe so long as you travel with us, lass. Come now, we've proved ourselves friendly and told you our names—what is your own?"

Mira looked from one to the other yet again. Somehow both she and the man seemed to be smaller, human rather than gigantic, though still very tall. She felt the tension begin to go out of her. "Mira. My name is Mira."

"Very well, then: Mira, Alea, and Gar." Alea nodded. "Can you tell us, lass, what you did that was so outrageous that Roketh would send these ghosts and riders after you?"

"I—I tried to escape," Mira admitted, lowering her gaze.

"Escape?" Alea's voice hardened. "By what right did he hold you in bondage?"

"Why, by his right as my lord." Mira looked up at Alea wide-eyed. "It was wrong of me to flee, for a serf must work for her lord, no matter who he is."

"Stuff and nonsense!" Alea snapped. "You belong to no one but yourself, lass, and don't ever let anyone tell you otherwise!"

"True," Gar said, "but it must have taken a powerful threat to make you leave your home and family."

"It did, sir." Mira lowered her gaze again. "Roketh sent . . . he sent his soldiers to bring me to his castle, and I have seen what happened to other girls who answered that summons—so I fled."

"As indeed you should!" Alea cried indignantly. "He had no business summoning you only for his own depraved pleasure, and you had every right to refuse—even if the only way to do that was to flee!"

She said it with so much heat that Mira wondered if she had a similar story to tell, but that heat warmed Mira's heart and made her think that perhaps she had done the right thing after all.

"These other women who had obeyed and gone to Roketh's castle," Gar reminded her. "What did happen to them?"

"Their eyes . . . their slumping shoulders . . . their . . ." Suddenly the horror of it overwhelmed her again, and Mira burst into tears once more.

Alea folded the young woman in her arms, murmuring, "Hush, dear, it's over, and he can't reach you now. Don't worry, whatever happened to those others won't happen to you. There, now, it will be all right."

Gar turned his face away, gazing down the road, then glancing at the forest to either side, then behind them. He seemed rather grim, as though this were an old and far too familiar tale.

Mira's sobs finally eased; she drew a little away from Alea and wiped her eyes on her sleeve, summoning the remnants of poise. "They . . . they will seek us here. . . ."

"Yes, but not back at our camp," Alea said. "Come, dear, we have a stew to heat."

Mira hung back. "The ghosts . . . they can find us by our thoughts. . . ."

"I don't think any of those specters are going to be terribly anxious to renew our acquaintance," Gar said with gentle amusement. "Let's go—we left the stew over the fire."

Alea cast him a sharp glance—she knew very well that he had damped the flames before he followed her. Still, what he had said was literally true—the stewpot was hanging over the campfire. It was simply not lit.

When they reached the campsite, though, she saw that the fire was lit, and the stew simmering gently. She cast a suspicious look at Gar, but he was all innocence. She grumbled under her breath about long-distance fire-lighting show-offs, then hastened to make Mira feel welcome. "Come now, dear, sit close to the flames—that's right. You'll feel better with a bit of stew in you. Where's that third bowl . . . ah, there." She pulled a wooden bowl out of her pack and ladled stew into it, then handed it to Mira and filled two more. "Gar, take the stewpot off the fire, will you? We have to boil water for tea."

Gar switched pots before he settled down with his own bowl and round of hard bread.

As they ate, Alea and Gar took turns asking questions, then answering her answers with little tales of their own, about the villages in which they had grown and the neighbors' eccentricities. Mira actually found herself laughing, though she would have sworn the last three days had made her forget how.

Before she knew it, she was talking like a waterfall, explaining to Gar and Alea what life was like in her village: the daily round of cleaning and tilling and mending and cooking; about Roketh and his guardsmen; about the cures he had performed when an epidemic seemed about to sweep the village and the punishments he had inflicted for disobedience.

Gar was interested in Roketh's battles with other magicians, and she told him what she had heard. Alea was interested in the ways in which the female magicians treated their serfs, so Mira told what she had heard about that, too. As she talked, though, the strain of the last few days lifted; she began to relax and, before she knew it, was fighting to keep her eyes open.

Alea saw it. "Time for you to sleep, I think, my dear. Here, you take this bed of pine boughs—you'll find it remarkably comfortable. No, don't argue—I can make another quickly enough, but truth to tell, I shan't need to, for Gar and I never sleep at the same time, one of us is always sitting up awake to keep the fire burning and to watch for . . . unwelcome company. No, now, sleep."

Mira protested but found that she was settling herself on the boughs as she did, and fell asleep as she was claiming that she could be comfortable enough on the hard ground.

"She probably could have been, too," Gar said, gazing at the sleeping woman. "She was tired enough for it."

"No reason to let her, though," Alea said sharply.

"No, of course not. What do you make of these ghosts, Alea? Other than a rumpled bedsheet, of course."

Alea shuddered. "Sleep with one of those things over me? No, thank you!" Then, more thoughtfully, "I don't think they're really the spirits of the dead."

"I would guess that some of the people here are telepaths, but don't know it," Gar said, "and are projecting their dreams and superstitions into others' minds—without the slightest idea they're doing it."

"But the ghosts have minds of their own," Alea objected.

"A public dream that's easier to start than to stop," Gar guessed.

Alea shook her head. "Too simple. The dreamers would still have to be dreaming to make the ghosts respond to the living people they encounter."

"A point," Gar admitted. He stared at the fire in thought, then asked, "Could they be a local life-form that developed a symbiosis with the colonists?"

"Symbiosis?" Alea looked up, frowning. "That happens when both life-forms gain something from each other. What would the colonists gain from having the specters take on their forms and personalities?"

"Immortality of a sort," Gar said, "though I'm sure the local spirits can't really absorb souls. If it exists, the soul has a completely different kind of reality from our universe of matter and energy."

"True," Alea countered, "but it does leave some very strong traces, such as life and personality."

"Strictly, a soul is life-force," Gar said thoughtfully, "and when it passes out of the body, perhaps it releases all the electrical energy patterns that it built up over the years—releases that part that belongs to our world, that is; it would take the spiritual energy, the memories and personality, with it."

"So the local ghosts can't gain the memories and thought patterns until a person dies," Alea said thoughtfully, "which means they're not really spirits."

"No, just some very diffuse form of matter," Gar said, "or perhaps a very concentrated form of energy; I know a physicist who claims that whether something is matter or energy depends on your point of view."

"Not mine," Alea protested. "Wouldn't it be the ghosts' viewpoint that matters?"

Gar shrugged. "What they're made of doesn't really signify anything. What's important is that they take on the shapes, personalities, and memories of people who have died. I wouldn't believe it if I hadn't seen them and heard their thoughts, but. . . ."

"Well, they weren't figments of your imagination," Alea told him. "I saw and heard them, too. For all practical purposes, they *are* the ghosts of dead people."

"Yes, and it would seem the local magicians can persuade them to do their dirty work. Which brings us to Mira."

"A local serf on the run, just as you hoped to find," Alea reminded. "But that first ghost's thought of fear wasn't the only one we heard. I felt a wave of sheer terror, and it wasn't what the ghost was projecting, it was the response it raised in Mira."

"Yes, and we weren't particularly trying to read minds at the time," Gar said. "She sent that through all by herself, so strongly that we couldn't ignore it—and I don't think she knew she was doing it."

"So, she's a telepath," Alea concluded.

"I wouldn't go that far," Gar said. "She doesn't seem to have read our minds, after all. She's definitely an empath though— able to feel others' emotions and project her own."

Alea frowned up at him. "Don't sound so shocked. All right, it's amazing, but if you found me, you shouldn't be surprised to find other mind readers."

"I suppose not," Gar said, "but I grew up with the idea that most of the galaxy's telepaths lived on my home planet, and even there they were rare."

"Maybe so," Alea answered, "but whoever told you that didn't know about Midgard—or Oldeira, as it turns out."

"No," Gar said, "I guess they didn't. I wonder if all the Lost Colonies have telepaths."

"Not all," Alea objected. "You've visited some of them."

"Yes, some." Gar recovered his assurance. "And SCENT has visited quite a few more; surely they would have reported finding telepaths. Still, it seems Gramarye isn't the only world to foster espers. I'm going to have to approach other planets with an open mind."

"Not too open," Alea cautioned. "It might be better to keep your shield up."

"Yes, it might." Gar smiled, amused. "Though not so vital as it might be, with your shield to guard my back."

"Is that all I am to you—a shield-companion?" Alea couldn't keep the bitterness from her voice.

"Only?" Gar stared. "There's just one way people can be closer! What do you mean, 'only'?"

But Alea fastened on the first statement. "One way? What's Number One?"

A shadow crossed Gar's face; he turned away. "One that's closed to me." He smoothed his expression as he turned back to her. "I rejoice in the friendships I can know, and delight in the presence of so excellent a woman as my companion."

Alea stared, dazed by the compliment but feeling a certain hollowness within her in spite of it. It was flattering to realize that if he were attracted to her, it was quite literally for her mind, or rather her telepathic abilities. Nonetheless, she was surprised to realize that she felt rather chagrined. That surprise bred fear, which sharpened her tone as she said, "But Mira doesn't have such a shield and doesn't know how to make one yet. Do you think her empathic ability attracted the ghosts?"

"No," Gar said slowly, "I think her magical lord of the manor sicced them on her. But I take your point: her psionic talent probably helped them to home in on her." He gave her a sudden grin. "No need to ask how you managed to banish them. I don't expect they're used to the intensity of anger you aimed at them."

Alea turned her head a little to the side, watching him out of the corner of her eye. "Are you sure my capacity for anger is a good thing?"

"That," Gar said gravely, "depends entirely on who you choose as a target . . . and why," he added as an afterthought.

"Well, there was a good deal of indignation in it too," she told him. "After all, they had no right to pick on that poor girl."

"They certainly did not," Gar agreed, "but how did you know telepathy would banish them?"

Alea stared at him, momentarily at a loss. Then she said, "It only made sense. If they implanted fear in their victims by telepathy, they should have been vulnerable to it themselves." A need for honesty made her add, "Of course, I didn't think that through before I acted."

"Yes, you did," Gar said. "You just didn't put it into words—you understood it all in an instant." His smile was slight, but his eyes glowed at her.

Alea looked away, embarrassed. "I didn't know why I was so sure aiming my anger at them would work—I just knew it would."

"As indeed it did," Gar said. "I suspect that it was your self-confidence that daunted them as much as your rage."

Alea frowned. "You mean they're all bluff?"

"No, all thought," Gar said, "even if they are made of gossamer. Their essence is mind-energy; they're creatures of idea—mental constructs."

"And if they're shaped by people's minds, they're vulnerable to them." Alea nodded.

"Therefore they should be attracted by telepathy. I see how you worked it out." Gar nodded. "Let's try the experiment."

"What experiment?" Alea asked in alarm.

But Gar was gazing off into the night. She could feel the pressure of his thoughts, hear his unvoiced words: *Here I am—here, for all to see. Come find me if you will and match me thought for thought.*

Alea leaped to her feet. "You're crazy! You have no idea what might answer that call! Gar, *stop!*"

But he didn't; he was already in a trance in which the world of thought seemed more real than the world of the body. She had to distract him, make him break off that mental searchlight. In a panic, she leaned forward and planted her lips squarely on his. She knelt frozen, shocked by her own brazen conduct, then was amazed by how good his lips felt, how surprisingly soft; they almost seemed to swell, to turn outward, to become sensuous instead of the thin gash he showed the world. His arms came around her; the kiss deepened, and she knew with certainty that he was no longer issuing his mental challenge. The kiss had served its purpose. That was enough.

The trouble was, she didn't want to stop.

5

A moan of grief swelled out of the night and wrapped them
in its lament. Startled, they broke apart, and Alea knelt
trembling, frightened, looking up. A ghost towered over them,
an amorphous thing with upright ovals for eyes and a larger one
for a mouth, arms spread wide in grief, and Alea told herself it
was the specter that made her tremble. Yes, that was it. Surely.

The ghost drifted closer, moaning, arms uplifted—in sup-
plication, Alea realized with a shock, then wondered how she
knew.

"Beware!" Mira called, awakened by the moans, her voice
shaking. "It is a wild ghost, a half ghost! It will be hungry."

The ghost turned away, looking back over the slope that
passed for a shoulder, and began to float away from them, its
moan becoming piteous. "Such are their tricks!" Mira cried. "It
will beguile you into following it, lead you into a mire, then wait
for you to sink and die so that it may feed upon your spirit!"

"We'll have to be very careful, then." Gar stood, gaze fixed
on the ghost. "Will you come with us, damsel? It might not be
safe for you here alone. Or perhaps Alea could stay with you."

"And let you go chasing a will-o'-the-wisp into some swamp?" Alea snapped. "Not a chance!" She glared at the fire; it shrank a little, then flared up again. "Oh, be dimmed to you!" she snapped, and scooped dirt on the flames. They went out, but smoke spiraled up; she tossed more dirt to smother it completely, then pushed herself to her feet, resolving to practice her telekinesis. "Come, lass," she said to Mira. "We can't let him go hunting by himself—there's no telling what kind of trouble he'll find!"

Trembling, Mira stood and followed them.

The ghost drifted away, its tone changing to one of relief, then to worry. It flitted into the trees.

"I'll watch the ghost," Alea snapped. "You watch the ground."

"And I shall watch before and behind us." Mira pressed close but kept going, trembling but resolute.

They went into the trees, watching every step. The ghost waited until they were about ten feet away, then drifted onward, staying close enough so that its glow could show them roots and rocks in their path.

"Strange, for a wild ghost." Mira frowned. "They don't usually help you see your way."

"It may only be half-formed," Gar said, "but it's not half-smart."

"Let's reserve judgment on that, shall we?" Alea asked, "We haven't come to the mire yet."

Mira was deeply puzzled. Ghosts didn't behave like this, trying to keep you from falling—they wanted to trap you, or so everyone said. Why did this one seem to care about them? Why did it sound worried?

They followed the ghost for half an hour before she discovered the reason. The phantom stopped by a huge old oak, with leaves so thick the ground was bare all around it. The tree was so old that a waist-high root bulged out of the earth—and beneath that root huddled a man, a young man. The ghost's glow showed her a strained, frightened, but very handsome face—one smudged with dirt from a dozen falls, a cheek swollen with a bruise, but the large eyes faced them bravely and the square chin firmed with determination that did not quite hide its dimple. His lips were full and supple, promising a sensuous nature. His nose was straight, his forehead high, and his hair tousled. Looking upon him, Mira felt something turn over within her, and knew it was her heart trying to escape to him.

The ghost hovered near the young man, its moan turning to a plea. Gar came slowly to stand across from it, gazing down at the lad. "It would seem our specter has a friend."

"A friend who needs help," Alea agreed. "No wonder it wanted to make sure we came here safely."

They stood close enough so that the ghost-glow fell full upon them, and the young man glanced at Gar, then Alea, but his gaze went past them both to Mira, and his eyes widened in awe. She stirred uncomfortably—why was he staring so?

"I had thought there were no goddesses," the young man breathed, "but here is one glowing before me!"

"Enough of pretty speeches, boy." Alea sounded nettled, perhaps because he had not spoken to her. "What is your name, and how have you come here?"

The young man hesitated, then said, "My lord lost a battle and was slain. I tore off my livery and fled. The ghosts shielded me from the enemy's soldiers, but I lost my way."

Mira was amazed. He must be a very good man indeed for ghosts to care for him.

"But your name?" Alea pressed.

"He fears we will use it to work magic against him," Gar told her. "Come, lad, do we look like magicians?"

Mira had to admit that they didn't, though she knew that

they were, but she also knew she could trust them, so she did not betray them to the young man.

"You do not," he admitted. "My name is Blaize."

"A good name." Gar reached down. "Come, lad, on your feet—or have you turned your ankle?"

"No." Blaize took Gar's hand and pulled himself upright. "I hide only for fear of Pilochin's guards."

He wore a peasant's tunic and leggins, but not a plowman's buskins—his feet were cased in well-made boots, like a soldier's. Mira's heart went out to him—a poor serf, pressed into service as she had been, though his duties hadn't been as degrading as those Roketh had intended for her. They might, though, have been just as shattering, or even fatal. She stepped up to take his arm. "You are favoring that ankle. Will it hold your weight?"

Blaize turned to her in surprise, and Mira saw the awe and admiration in his eyes. She began to glow inside and it must have showed in her face, for his gaze was riveted to hers, and his eyes seemed to expand to become the world. Mira shook off the trance, looking down at his foot. "Come now, stand on it."

"Oh, I can walk." To prove it, Blaize took a few steps, though with a slight limp.

"You are hiding pain," Mira accused. "Come, lean on my shoulder." She looked up at Alea and Gar. "He needs warmth and hot broth."

"Yes, he does," Alea said, amused, but Gar only nodded gravely and turned away. "Come."

"Call if we go too swiftly for you," Alea told Mira, "and we'll slow down." Then she turned away to walk beside Gar.

They kept their pace slow and Mira found she and Blaize were able to match it. "Did your lord press you into his service, or did you volunteer?"

"Volunteered, in a way." Blaize gave her a sickly grin. "I ran away, found a magician who was kind to his peasants, and enlisted in his service."

Mira's eyes widened, and her insides flipped over again. "That was dangerous—and very brave."

Blaize shrugged off the praise, embarrassed. "I could not stay to see my family ground down further every day, and I would rather have died than serve their lord."

"You might have died indeed!" Mira exclaimed. She had heard of such daring, but only rarely—if a serf could escape and take service with another magician, his old lord had to let him go; custom as well as prudence dictated such restraint, for there was no reason to go to war over a single runaway, especially since his new lord might prove stronger. "Were you lucky or shrewd? Most who try to escape are usually caught and flogged within an inch of their lives!"

"Sometimes past that," Blaize said grimly. "I've heard of men dying under the lash."

"Yes, and I've heard of others whom the guards have killed outright before they could find a new magician to accept their service! You were very lucky—and very brave." Her eyes shone.

"I was lucky indeed," Blaize said fervently, "though there was some sense in it, too. I knew which magician I sought before I fled, you see."

"You did! But—but I thought that all lords were equally cruel. What point is there in escaping one only to find another who is just as bad?"

"But I had heard of Arnogle and his kindness before I escaped," Blaize told her.

"Oh . . . Arnogle. Yes." Mira's gaze strayed. Everyone had heard of Arnogle and his generosity. "But he is not the strongest of magicians, is he?"

She regretted the words the moment she'd said them, even more when she saw Blaize wince with the pain of memory. "He was not, alas—though he proved quite a bit stronger with me to aid him."

"Aid him!" Mira froze. "Aid him in what way?"

"By summoning ghosts," Blaize explained. "I could do that much, but I could scarcely do anything with them at all once they had come." He gave her a sardonic smile. "I think that was why my old lord let me escape—he was tired of having ghosts hanging about the village with nothing to do. There was always the chance they would turn mischievous, you see."

"I see indeed!" Mira dropped his arm as though it were fire-hot. "You were Arnogle's apprentice!"

"Why, yes." Blaize's eyes widened. "What sort of service did you think I meant?"

"As a guard, of course!" Mira backed away, trembling "What did you think to do once you had become a magician in your own right—capture some peasants to toil for you, whip them when you were bored, and summon their daughters to your bed whenever it pleased you?"

"Not at all!" Blaize said, startled. "I meant to overthrow my old lord and govern his peasants with kindness and generosity!"

"Indeed! And how long would it have been before you began to enjoy the power of making others cringe?" Mira whirled to Alea and Gar. "Send him away! It was not a soldier's uniform he cast away in his flight—it was a socerer's robe and tall pointed hat! He is one of them, he is a sorcerer's apprentice!"

The two tall people stopped, turning to her in surprise. "Is he really?" Alea asked.

Blaize stared at her, wounded. "An apprentice I am, and would have become a magician if my master had not been slain in this battle. Is that so bad a thing?"

"Yes," Mira snapped. "Magicians make people suffer and fear

them, then force them to do things they don't want to do, things they know are wrong!"

Alea looked at her in surprise, then in sympathy, and Mira knew the tall woman had a past much like her own. She said, though, "A man can be a magician and still be good."

Too late, Mira remembered that these two were magicians themselves, but magicians from far away. "Not in this land!"

"Most magicians are tyrants," Blaize agreed, "but my master was not. His peasants loved him."

"They still were peasants!"

"Yes, but they lived comfortably, He was a good man and a kind lord."

"How long would he have remained so?" Mira demanded. "Even a magician who means to be good gives in to temptation, a little at first, then more and more, until he becomes as wicked as any!"

"There are always a few who manage to withstand the lure of corruption," Gar said quietly. "He deserves his chance to prove his good will. Certainly he has seen a good example, if his master did indeed rule his peasants with justice and kindness."

"He did, and they were happy." Blaize looked away, shivering. "Alas for them! How shall they fare, now that Pilochin has conquered them?"

Mira shivered, too, at the foul name. "I have heard of Pilochin. He burns people."

"He is a fire-caster," Blaize said grimly. "He burned my master Arnogle and all his guards."

A shoot of pity sprouted in Mira's heart but she did her best to pluck it out. "Why, then, are you left alive?"

"I scarcely know." Blaize's gaze drifted away, face racked with grief and guilt. "My ghost warned me at the last second; I drew back and shouted a warning to Arnogle, but it was too late."

Mira stared. "You are a ghost-leader! No wonder the specter led us to you!"

"I called it up and beseeched it to find me help," Blaize admitted. "It is a very friendly ghost and took pity on me."

"Friendly to you!" Mira turned to Alea and Gar. "For anyone else, this specter would have stood by and waited for him to die so that it could gobble his spirit and turn itself into his ghost! He must be a powerful magician indeed to be able to command it to do his will!"

"I did not command," Blaize protested, "only beseeched and persuaded."

"What did you promise to give it in return?" Mira snapped. "The life of one of the people it brought to aid you?"

Alea stiffened. Gar's eyes gleamed.

"I promised it nothing," Blaize said indignantly. "I made it proud to be what it is—a wild ghost, unshaped by human will."

"Human will! It is the ghost who swallows the human, not the human the ghost!"

"Sometimes," Blaize said. "Most often, though, the dying spirit seizes upon a ghost as a way to hold on to life. The ghost does not enjoy the experience and is itself extinguished, swallowed up by the human personality."

"Then why do ghosts cluster around a deathbed?" Mira demanded.

"Because that is when the human spirit cries out," Blaize told her, "some for Heaven, because they have lived long and fully and are ready to die; some because life has tortured them and they welcome death; but many because they have enjoyed life and wish to hold to it, no matter what the cost—the cost to others, at least."

Mira stared. "I have never heard any of this."

"Few have," Blaize said, "only ghost-leaders, and who would believe us if we told?"

Mira was silent, disconcerted.

Blaize smiled sadly. "Even you yourself. Even when I have told you, you do not believe me."

"I do not!" Mira said hotly. "It is a ghost-leader's lie, to betray us into the hands of your phantoms!"

"I would do no such thing," Blaize protested, "and if you do not wish to make a ghost of yourself, they would not harm you in any case."

"Oh, so all the ghosts are harmless, are they?"

"Not all," Blaize admitted, "especially those who have become shadows of wicked persons. The wild ghosts, though, are mostly peaceful things who avoid humans unless they feel us call."

"Peaceful! Aye, the peace of the grave!"

"There is peace in the grave indeed," Blaize said gravely, "and all human souls pass to the Afterlife, but many leave behind their reflections as they go, shadows impressed on wild ghosts—prey more often than hunters."

"Pray indeed, to save us from them!"

"I have, and have saved nine ghosts already from enslavement to a human's will."

"Saved the people's spirits from being swallowed by the ghosts, you mean!"

"Some," Blaize admitted, "those who had no wish to hold on to this world. The others I thwarted in their desire to stay here."

"To stay! Who would wish to stay if they could only look upon the world from a ghost's eyes, could only look upon food and love and children but never taste or feel or touch? If this is your mercy, save me from it—and from any who argue for the goodness of ghosts!" Mira spun on her heel and stalked away, past Alea and Gar, back the way they had come.

"You had best make sure she comes safe to the campsite,"

Gar said. "In the mood she's in, she could wander quite far from it and lose herself in the wood."

"I wouldn't know the way myself if I hadn't kicked rocks as we went." Alea picked up a fallen branch. "I'll need some light—other than an obliging ghost, I mean. I don't think Mira would take well to such company right now."

"Indeed she would not." Gar stared at the dead wood for a few seconds. It burst into flame.

"You are a fire-caster!" Blaize cried, shrinking back.

"If I have to be," Gar said, frowning. "Go quickly, Alea. She'll lose herself in another minute."

"Hasn't she already?" But Alea didn't stay to explain what she meant.

Gar turned toward Blaize, who cowered against a trunk, hands up to ward as his lips moved soundlessly. Ghosts seemed to rise from the very ground, drifted in from the trees, most shapeless and moaning, one or two in jerkins and hose, bows in their hands and quivers of arrows on their backs.

"Who are you who imperils our wood?" one of them demanded.

"I am Gar Pike, and I cry the sanctuary of the greenwood," Gar said, "even as you did in life, or I miss my guess."

"We were outlaws, aye, and ever ready to protect poor folk such as ourselves." The other human form gave Gar a nasty grin. "If any magic-lord was foolish enough to come within our forest, we dealt with him as best we could, and quickly, too."

"An arrow through the breast," Gar interpreted, "while another of you warned all wild ghosts away. Or did you find a way to slay a tyrant's ghost?"

"No need—the shadows of those who had guarded the woodland before us held the wild ones back." The first outlaw frowned. "What manner of man are you, who speaks with ghosts?"

"Why, he is a magician, Ranulf!" the other outlaw said. "Who else could talk to us without fear?"

"A magician from far away, yes," Gar said, "and a lord—but not of any estate, and surely I hold no lands here."

"You seek them, then." Ranulf drifted closer, his manner threatening.

"I seek to free peasants from cruel lords, yes," Gar said, "but I have no wish to stay in one place long enough to be lord of a manor."

The second outlaw frowned. "I hear his heart's desire, Conn, and though it seeks what it does not know, it seeks not power."

"He is sincere," Ranulf agreed. He turned to Blaize. "Why did you call us, man? This big fellow means you no harm, means only to aid you."

"He—he is a fire-caster!" Blaize stared at Gar. "And a ghost-leader, too—but that cannot be! No fire-caster has ever been a ghost-leader, save the vile Roketh!"

"I am both, and have many other magical gifts besides," Gar told him. "Perhaps you have the talent to learn some of them."

"Perhaps." Blaize wavered visibly. "That is a bribe, is it not? Bait for a trap?"

"The promise of knowledge has lured better men than either of us," Gar told him, "but I do not use it so—the greed for learning is your own. I didn't put it there. And I don't promise to teach you, for I don't *know* whether you have the talent for it. But I will protect you from the magician who pursues you, aye, protect you as well as I can."

"What good will that do?" Blaize's shoulders sagged. "No magician will accept an apprentice whose magician has died— they will think I am no use if I could not help defend my master. I cannot become a serf again, because no lord will trust me not to be a spy, and my old lord would slay me out of hand as a traitor. I may as well lie down upon the ground and die!"

"If you really believed that, you wouldn't have asked a ghost to find help for you." Gar thumped the young man on the back. "Have hope! There is life here yet, and you're young. As long as you stay alive, you may stumble across a new chance—and you have, for if you have as much talent as you say and need a teacher, you've found one."

"Why?" Blaize stared at Gar, unable to believe in the rescue of his hopes. "Why should you care about me?"

"Because I need all the friends I can gather," Gar told him, "especially if I intend to free any of the serfs of this land. I may have magic, but I'm also an outlander who needs someone who knows this country."

Now, Blaize could have protested that Gar seemed far more worldly than himself, but the lure of learning was too strong for him. He stepped away from the tree trunk, saying, "Knowledge for knowledge? Magic for local guidance?"

"Knowledge, yes," Gar said. "As to magic, you'll have to see to that yourself. Can you use the knowledge I give you, or will it simply be interesting for its own sake?"

"I shall give you any help I can," Blaize promised.

"A bargain, then." Gar clasped his hand, then turned away. "We must go quickly, now. The ladies have a long head start."

Blaize fell in beside him, not even noticing that the tall man shortened his strides to match Blaize's. He was too much absorbed in his misery; the delight at the thought of new knowledge had faded, submerged under a vision of green eyes and auburn hair. Why had Mira's interest turned to hatred at the mere mention that he was a magician's apprentice? Why was she so quick to think him evil? How could he win her regard again?

Behind them, the wild ghosts faded back into forest and brush, sensing they were no longer needed, but Ranulf nudged Conn in his mistlike ribs and nodded toward the besotted and dejected young man. Conn answered with a wink and a grin. Together, the two outlaw ghosts drifted along behind the living men.

Conn and Ranulf faded from sight when Gar and Blaize came to the campsite, though. If Blaize had paid attention, he would have known they were there simply by the feel of their presence—but he had room for nothing in his mind but the sight of Mira, her graceful movements and delicate beauty.

Gar and Alea could have sensed the ghosts, too, if they'd known what the feeling meant. As it was, they did the best they could to soothe the two young people with tea, then stew, then saw them to sleep on beds of pine boughs. When they were sure the two slept, Alea looked up across the fire at Gar and said, "A runaway serf girl escaping her lord's command to warm his bed, and a masterless man who is probably the only one of his teacher's retinue left alive. How are we supposed to keep them safe?"

6

W ell asked," Gar said. "Her lord and his enemy have probably both sent hunters after them. It doesn't help that they're both sure of defeat."

"Yes, they seem to be convinced they're only postponing the inevitable," Alea said with a wry smile. "Mira is quite sure that some magician somewhere will claim her for his plaything. Probably right, too—she is a beautiful creature, and every inch of this land seems to belong to one magician or another."

"True—so Blaize is convinced his master's enemy will find him sooner or later, and even if he doesn't, the boy will have no future but that of an outlaw." Gar sighed and shook his head. "They've both lost their battles already, and for no better reason than being convinced they can't win."

"They might at least try," Alea grumbled, "but it looks as though we'll have to do their trying for them."

"I don't think they're all that rare, either," Gar said. "I think we can assume that if they're so thoroughly cowed, all the people are—or most of them, at least."

"Yes, we do seem to have stumbled across two of the more

spirited ones," Alea admitted. "They both had the nerve to try to escape—but where to? There doesn't really seem to be any safe place for them, unless you count the greenwood."

"The bandits there will probably be just as cruel as the lords." Gar looked up, frowning around at the trees. "I could have sworn I heard somebody clear his throat."

"Probably just some animal with an odd kind of cry," Alea said. "Of course, you never know. The bandits might be sympathetic."

"Even if they are, it's a dangerous life," Gar said. "No, if there isn't any kind of refuge for these two, we'll have to make one."

Alea eyed him askance. "You're not thinking of building another resistance movement, are you?"

"Of course," Gar said in surprise.

"I was afraid of that," Alea sighed. "It was too much to hope you'd find a rebellion already simmering. Well, if you're going to start a revolution, you'd better sleep while you can. Good night."

"Good night?" Gar stared. "I always take first watch!"

"Yes, but it's the middle of the night, and that's when the second watch always starts." Alea grinned. "Too bad, soldier boy. My turn to stay awake."

Gar argued for only a few minutes before he gave in with a sigh and said, "Mind you wake me in four hours."

"And if I don't?"

"I'll wake myself, of course." Gar lay down and wrapped himself in his cloak. "Good night, Alea."

"Good night." She watched as he rolled over in his pine nest, broad shoulders rising up like a hill, and wondered when she had become so certain that her life was wrapped up in this reserved, distant man. Perhaps it was the stream of verbal assaults she had heaped on him in the year she had known him, and his never responding with anger, but only a deeper and deeper concern.

Concern for what? For her? Why should he be concerned for her instead of for himself? She felt a fluttering within her at the thought and tried to force it back. Surely it was the martial arts practice sessions that made him endure her, or the shared danger on the planet Brigante, her guarding his back, helping to achieve his goal—never mind that she had burned to overthrow the warlord as hotly as he.

She shook off the mood irritably and turned back to the fire. It was burning low; she added some more wood, then frowned at it, watching fairy castles build and transform into cities of crystal until, with a start, she jerked her gaze to the dark woods about her, wondering how much time had passed while she rested in trance—minutes or hours?

A huge round silhouette bulked out of the night. Alea rose clutching her quarterstaff, heart in her throat, ready to scream for Gar, but the huge form drifted into the firelight and with a sigh of relief she recognized Evanescent.

With recognition came memory—and the realization of its loss. "You made me forget you again," she accused.

"Of course," the alien said, sitting its stunted body down with feline grace. "What would your male think if you'd told him you had long cozy chats with a huge-headed catlike telepathic alien?"

"He'd believe me in an instant," Alea snapped, "and they're not cozy chats, more like prickly inquisitions. Besides, he's not *my* male."

"Never mind, dear, you'll admit it some day," Evanescent said. "You might offer a body a dish of tea, you know."

Alea stared. "When did you begin drinking tea?" She frowned. "Come to that, what are you doing here? You're one of Brigante's natives, and this is the planet Oldeira."

"I decided to see the new worlds you planned to visit,"

Evanescent said. "Life has become dull this last century or two, but you and your . . . Gar livened it up immensely. I came along to see if you were as much fun on somebody else's planet as on my own."

Alea knew that Brigante rightly belonged to Evanescent and her kind, and that they tolerated the Terran colonists for amusement. "I'm glad to know we're so interesting," she said with irony she hoped Evanescent would detect. "Really, though, I was asking how you had traveled ten light-years."

"I stowed away in the cargo hold of your spaceship, of course, and tried brewing some of the tea I found there—while the robot wasn't looking, that is."

"Herkimer is always looking—everywhere on his ship and around it!"

"Not when I encourage him not to." Evanescent gave her a toothy smile. "Of course, I had to search your male's mind to learn what to do with those funny little leaves. I quite liked the flavor."

"I told you, he's not mine." Alea held on to her patience only by great effort. "Call him Gar, at least. You might give me bad ideas."

"Or good ones, but you're not recovered enough for those yet." Evanescent stared at the bark kettle.

Alea sighed, taking the hint and swinging it over the fire again. She poured in more water from her canteen. "This will take a while to boil, you know."

"I can wait," the alien said equably.

She could indeed, as Alea well knew. "We might wake Gar and the youngsters with our talking."

"No need for concern there," Evanescent assured her. "I've seen to it they'll sleep soundly till we're done—and you don't need to worry about predators, human or animal."

"No, I don't think any will come near while you're around."

Alea eyed Evanescent's double row of shark's teeth. Curiously, she herself wasn't at all afraid, even though she had some idea of Evanescent's powers. As soon as she saw the alien, of course, Alea remembered all their earlier conversations—and remembered also that as soon as those chats had ended, she had forgotten about them completely. No doubt she would forget this one, too, though she would act on the ideas Evanescent gave her, thinking them her own. The thought of such power should have been daunting, but perversely Alea only felt indignation. She wondered if she were really that brave or if it were only more of the alien's manipulation.

The thought made her wonder about her own strength of mind. "It wasn't me alone who banished those ghosts, was it?"

"I did give you a bit of help," Evanescent admitted, "though only by strengthening your mental thrust a bit. The anger was yours."

"I suppose that's reassuring," Alea said, then frowned. "My waking mind may have forgotten, but there was some memory you buried in me that made me certain I would be able to command those specters, wasn't there?"

"Was, and is," Evanescent assured her. "Don't worry, dear. You'll always be confident of your ability to deal with any situation I can handle."

Alea wasn't certain she liked that idea, but since she couldn't do much about it, she decided to enjoy the advantages. "The situations I'm likely to encounter are difficulties with local magicians. Can you deal with them?"

"One or two at a time," Evanescent said judiciously. "Of course, with your friend Gar helping out, the three of us together should be able to cope with five or six of the locals. Their psi power isn't really all that strong, you know."

"Strong enough to tyrannize their serfs!" Alea snapped.

"That takes cleverness and ruthlessness, not telepathy,"

Evanescent told her. "I've surveyed three kinds of magicians so far, and the fire-casters don't have any psi power at all."

Alea stared. "Then how—?"

"They kept alive one element of Terran technology," Evanescent explained, "and guard its secret closely. They teach their apprentices how to work the flamethrowers, but even if those apprentices are their sons, they don't teach them how to make the fuel, or where to find the rock-oil from which they make it. That secret they pass on only when they're dying."

"Untrusting and manipulative," Alea interpreted. "Greedy, too, if the look of their serfs is anything to go by. Their clothes are patched and worn and the few new garments they have are very obviously homemade."

"They're barely getting by," Evanescent said, "and don't have much time to spare for spinning fine thread or weaving soft cloth. But you have to admit the lords clothe their soldiers well."

"Yes, and give them very shiny weapons, too! They're unfeeling and insensitive, though, if Mira's predicament is at all common."

"The magicians are greedy for things other than money," Evanescent agreed. "All in all, I would have to say that if you and Gar wish to devote a year or so to destroying their power, you would be spending the time well."

"I've seen people in worse straits," Alea said, "but these are surely bad enough to justify our butting in." She frowned. "How, though? We've dealt with a warlord before, and Herkimer has told me how Gar and his friend Dirk overthrew several tyrants, but none of them were magical! How do you fight a force you can't see?"

"Why, with belief in *other* powers you can't see." Evanescent smiled, a disconcerting sight in itself. "Do you remember Brigante's sages?"

"Why, yes," Alea said slowly. "They led the people in harmony and cooperation, healing minds and hearts."

"These magicians are just as much warlords as the bandit chieftain on Brigante wished to become," Evanescent pointed out, "though considering their mode of fighting, perhaps we should say 'magic-lords' instead of 'warlords.' Anything that makes people of different estates join together in any way should trouble the lords of those estates considerably."

"Especially if that thing is a way of thinking that isn't really a religion," Alea said, smiling, "but is so peaceable that it gives them no excuse for oppressing it."

"I don't think these magic-lords are the sort to require an excuse," Evanescent said thoughtfully, "but I do think even they would have trouble finding grounds to fight a philosophy until it had become too widespread to be exterminated."

"A notion definitely worth considering," Alea said with a smile, "especially if that religion had some physical disciplines that could very easily be turned into a system of fighting."

"I would be careful to hide the implications," Evanescent warned, "especially if you were tempted to make that philosophy prove itself by making things happen magically."

"Yes, any kind of magic would be grounds for local lords to stamp it out," Alea agreed. "I've learned that all governments depend on a monopoly of violence, but this is the first one I've ever heard of that depends on a monopoly of magic."

"Major magics, at least," Evanescent qualified. "Little tricks would pass unnoticed, but you never know which minor illusion will prove its power."

Alea heard an owl hoot behind her, then come rushing in a flutter of feathers. She turned to look just as the bird tilted its path to climb over her head. Its wings spanned four feet and its body had to be eighteen inches long at least. She turned frontward again to watch it climb, using the rising air from her fire as a spiral ladder. When it had disappeared into the night, she lowered her gaze, looking at the empty woods about her as a good sentry should, but the clearing was empty except for herself, her three companions, and their fire. Nothing else stirred, and she admitted to herself that she had become very sleepy.

Still, that was a good idea that had come to her in midnight musings. Second watch was lonely, but it was good for meditation. When nothing happened, though, it did make you feel like sleeping, and surely she had watched for four hours at least. She rose and went to wake Gar, looking forward to taking his place on the pine-bough pallet. The big lug would have warmed it well for her, if he had done nothing else this night.

He came awake instantly, starting up from sleep. "Trouble?"

"Not a bit," Alea told him. "Nothing moved except an owl that dive-bombed my head. Boring night. It's all yours."

She woke at first light while the younger people still slept. Over the first cup of tea she told Gar her idea, keeping her voice low. "The sages of Brigante showed us that philosophy and good example could work in place of a government, after all."

"Yes, when combined with village councils and enforced by a secret society." Gar's smile was tight with irony. "Still, it's a good idea—in a society like this one, it could be just the rallying point the people need."

"And by the time the movement is big enough to worry the magicians, it will be too big for them to stop," Alea said triumphantly.

"I wouldn't be so sure," Gar said. "Never underestimate the power of old-fashioned violence. But we might be able to mix in some self-defense lessons."

"You mean by teaching martial arts as part of the philosophy?"

"Why not? Some teachers say Tae Kwon Do is philosophy in action, after all. More to the point, Kung Fu came out of the Taoist monasteries, and that's the kind of thought system we'd be using here."

"Why Taoism?" Alea asked with a frown. "And how will we learn about it?"

"We'll tell Herkimer to print out copies of the books and drop them to us at night. As to why, it's because the Taoist sages are the ones who came up with the idea of a benign anarchy, one that would work by the peasants wanting to imitate the sage, who lived high on his mountain in the wilderness. Watching him, they would naturally want to live in harmony with their neighbors and their environment."

Alea gave a short laugh. "They forgot about human greed and lust for power."

"We all have our blind spots," Gar said, "but it was a noble ideal."

"What noble ideal? What could wash away human greed?"

They looked up to see Mira rising from her pine boughs and Blaize levering himself up on an elbow, blinking sleep out of his eyes.

"A philosophy," Alea answered, "a set of ideas that all fit together. If enough people believe in them, they can shape a whole society."

"Can they really?" Mira asked doubtfully.

"Somewhat," Gar said. "Monks and priests in all cultures have made them less violent than they might have been. The Greek philosophers invented a system of logic that grew into modern science and changed the world into a place of marvels. Confucian scholars invented a civil service system that made Chinese civilization last more than two thousand years. . . . The list goes on. The way we think can help change the way we live, yes."

Mira frowned. "Who were the Greeks? And the Confucians? What is Chinese? What is a civil service?"

"One question at a time," Gar said with a smile that would have been a laugh in another man. He began to explain. When he ran out of breath, Alea took over, then Gar again, then Alea.

Blaize listened, dazed, as Mira asked question after question. He was amazed at the panorama of marvels that Gar and Alea opened before him, but amazed even more by the quickness of Mira's intelligence. Strangely, it made her seem even more attractive. *That's wrong*, he thought. *Only people's hearts and looks should make them attractive.* Nonetheless, he couldn't deny that his pulse beat faster with each question Mira asked, each incisive comment she made.

At last Alea turned to him and asked, "Don't you have any questions, Blaize?"

"Well, yes," he said, still feeling dazed. "What is this Dowism you mentioned?"

"Taoism," Gar corrected, softening the dental sound and emphasizing the dipthong. Blaize frowned, noticing the subtle difference in the sound of the word. Gar explained, "The Tao is the harmony and unity of everything that exists. If we can understand how it all fits together and find our places in that great grand Unity, we'll be happier in this life and become even more a part of it after we die."

Blaize frowned. "Is that like Heaven?"

"In a way," Gar said, "a way of living forever. You might not be aware of it as yourself, though."

"Then again, you might," Alea said, "but you'd realize that what you'd thought of as 'Blaize' was really just a small part of everything you really are."

"So it's a matter of trying to discover everything you can become?" Mira asked.

"That's part of it," Alea said warily.

A thrill passed through Blaize's whole body. She understood so quickly! Too quickly, more quickly than he—he wasn't good enough for her. Of course, that didn't matter, since she had come to hate him as soon as she'd learned he was an apprentice magician.

Still, it wasn't long before Gar threw up his hands in surrender and Alea said, "You've come to the limit of what we know, Mira. We'll quickly learn more though, I promise you. I think that before we start studying, you'd better find us a mountaintop where we can be sure of some peace."

The mountains weren't hard to find—they towered in the distance. The companions spent the day hiking toward them, sometimes in silence, sometimes with Alea talking to Mira or Gar. Blaize felt rather left out but reminded himself how lucky he was to have any company at all. Now and again, though, Gar and Alea would teach them a song, and they would all march singing, "I'll build me a desrick on Yandro. . . ." though Blaize had no idea what a desrick was or where Yandro might be. From the look on Mira's face, he doubted that she did, either.

The next morning, he woke to find Gar and Alea taking turns reading passages from a book while the tea water heated and the journeybread fried. The book, as it turned out, was the *Tao Te Ching*, which Gar told him meant *The Book of the Way of Virtue*. After breakfast they hiked up into the foothills. Over the midday meal they read more of the book, then discussed it as they climbed into the mountains. Soon the way grew too steep for talking, but when they pitched camp, Alea sat reading the book while Gar showed the younger folk how to pitch camp, light a campfire, and prepare a meal. The next morning, Alea supervised the camp while Gar read—a different book this time, by someone named Chang Tzu.

After four days, they had finally come near enough to the mountaintop so that Gar and Alea were willing to make a more or less permanent camp—but by this time, they were so deeply involved in discussing the ideas in the books that they left pitching camp to Blaize and Mira. That meant the two of them had to talk to each other, at least to the extent of "Fetch a bucket of water, will you?" or "Do you think these pine boughs are thick enough for a bed?" or even, "Here, let me try—I've always been good with flint and steel."

"Of course," Mira said with scorn, "you're a magician, aren't you?"

Blaize looked up in surprise, trying to conceal his hurt—he'd had a good deal of practice at that lately. "I'm not that kind of magician." He turned back to the pile of kindling and struck a spark into the dried moss. "Not apt to become *any* kind of magician now."

"Oh, you seem to deal well enough with ghosts."

"Well enough for what?" Blaize watched the moss catch and breathed on it until a little flame licked upward; then he dropped on some wood shavings and watched the flame grow until he could add kindling. As the little fire blossomed, he said, "I'll be able to call for help, yes, if the nearby ghosts are kind, but if we run into anything mean, I doubt I'll be able to talk it into leaving us alone."

"Don't worry, Alea can." Mira watched him wince with a certain satisfaction. "Maybe she can teach you how to drive away spirits."

"I've asked," Blaize said glumly. "All she could tell me was that she let them feel the force of her anger."

"Well, it worked. What's the matter? Can't you get angry?"

"Of course," Blaize said, surprised. "I just don't seem to be able to aim it the way she does."

"Well, maybe thinking of them as parts of the Tao will help," Mira said with a touch of sarcasm.

Blaize's gaze leaped up to hers. "Why, what a marvelous idea! Perhaps I can learn to be a magician, after all."

He turned back to the fire and the glow in his face wasn't just the reflection of the flames. With a sinking heart, Mira wondered what she had started.

She told herself she didn't need to worry, that Gar and Alea weren't really magicians, or at least, not the same kind as the lords, nowhere nearly as powerful. She managed to keep believing that until dinner was done, the plates and pot scrubbed and packed, and Gar sat down cross-legged some distance from the fire, back ramrod straight, though his whole body seemed relaxed. He set his hands on his knees and tilted his head up slightly, staring at the profusion of stars. This high on the mountain, what few trees there were, were low and scrawny, so the sky spread above them in a vast panorama, stars strewn across it like powder. Mira sneaked peeks at Gar watching the heavens as she lay down to sleep, but there was something about him that set her on edge, even though at last he closed his eyes. She nudged Alea and asked, "Does he sleep sitting up?"

"No," Alea told her. "He is trying to read his brother's mind."

Mira looked up at her, suddenly wary. "Where is his brother?"

Alea turned and pointed up into the northwest sky. "There."

7

M ira stared at the sky, feeling a prickle of dread running down her spine. She forced words through stiff lips. "How can he read a mind so distant when he is doing nothing?"

"His body may be doing nothing," Alea explained, "but his mind is very active. He is meditating."

"What is that?"

Blaize propped himself up on an elbow to listen.

"Meditating means freeing your mind to explore with sharpened focus," Alea explained. "You see connections in the world that our waking mind does not. In his case, the world he can't see is his homeland, halfway across the galaxy."

Mira frowned. "What is 'the galaxy'?"

"All that." Alea swept a hand across the heavens. "All the stars you can see, and a great many more besides. Do you see those two that seem to be almost joined?"

"The Twins? Of course," Mira said. "Everyone knows of them."

"Well, they're really one light-year apart," Alea explained.

"That's so far that if you set out to walk to it, then turned the journey over to your child when you died, and your child left it to your grandchild, by the time one of your descendants came there, thousands of years would have passed, and your memory would be only a name, if it survived at all."

Mira stared, awed by the immensity suddenly breaking upon her senses. "But—but if those two are so close together, how far apart is the Ranger's left shoulder from his right?" She pointed to a parallelogram of stars.

"Hundreds of light-years," Alea said. "If someone were to light a huge fire on his left shoulder, your great-great-great-great-great grandchildren would be the first to see it."

Blaize shivered at the thought, but his face was rapt as he gazed at the stars.

Mira shivered, too, feeling suddenly alone and tiny, lost among the constellations. The old, familiar, friendly stars suddenly seemed cold and alien, and incredibly distant.

"Each of those stars is a sun," Alea explained, "like the bright ball that lights the day here and gives you its warmth and light."

"A sun?" Mira stared. "But there is only one sun, above the world! They can't be suns—they are too small!"

"They only seem small because they are so far away," Alea answered, "and they don't hang above the world, for worlds are balls of rock and earth and swing around their suns in endless circles."

Mira's eyes mirrored the horde of stars above her. "You mean each of those stars has a world?"

"No, only a few," Alea explained, "but that 'few,' when there are so many stars, means thousands."

Mira's mind reeled at the idea of thousands of worlds like her own, filled with warmth and flowers and animals and people, falling in love and marrying and living out their lives struggling to rear their children without starving.

"Do you see that river of stars that slants across the heavens?" Alea asked.

"The Waterfall of the Gods? Of course."

"That is really the far side of the galaxy," Alea explained.

Mira paled. "You mean Gar is trying to reach one of *those* stars with his mind?"

"No, the star he seeks is much closer, only two hundred thirty-four light-years away." Alea pointed at a patch of darkness between the Wagon and the Hoe. "It's somewhere in that part of the sky, but its sun is too small to see."

"Why does he want to reach so small a world with his mind?" Mira whispered.

"To talk to his little brother there," Alea explained. "He can reach across that gulf with his mind and read Gregory's thoughts."

Now Mira began to tremble. "Can his brother's mind reach here to us?"

"We think so," Alea said. "That's what Gar is trying to find out right now. He tells me I'll be able to do it someday, too, if I keep practicing." She leaned closer, her tone dropping in confidence. "I don't believe him, though. I think it takes two to forge that kind of link—and I don't have a brother or sister."

"Except Gar," Mira murmured, eyes on the stars, not really thinking—so she didn't notice how long Alea hesitated before she said, "Yes. Except for Gar."

"He can teach me magic." Blaize breathed, gazing at Gar with worshipful eyes. Then he transferred the same look to Alea. "So can you, if you will."

"Learn the Tao first," Alea said. "Then we'll talk about magic."

Mira felt a sudden determination to do exactly that.

• • •

They learned well enough in the little time that Alea and Gar were free to talk with them; for the next several days they seemed to be always reading and asked Mira and Blaize to do the chores of the camp for them. Mira complied, though warily, as though expecting them to turn into dragons the moment she turned her back. Blaize did his tasks cheerfully—after all, he had been fetching and carrying for Arnogle for years. Besides, if Gar had turned into a dragon, Blaize would only have stared and marveled.

In the afternoons, the two adventurers took turns; one would meditate while the other tried to teach the younger people about the Tao and how people behaved if they tried to follow that Way.

Gar explained that the ancient sages had really believed that if everybody lived in villages and each village had a sage living nearby, then the people would follow the example of the sages, treating each other with kindness and trying to settle their differences without anger or violence. Blaize found that he couldn't accept the idea. "What if another village didn't believe in the Way or wish to follow their sage? Wouldn't they try to conquer the neighboring villages and take everything they had, even the women and children?"

"Not if *everyone* believed in the Tao and tried to live like a sage," Gar answered.

"But that could never happen!" Blaize protested. "All it would take would be one person who didn't believe—especially if that person were a powerful magician. Then he would try to build up an army and use his powers to enslave everybody else."

Gar looked sharply at him. "Is that how your world came to be divided up between magic-lords?"

"I don't really know," Blaize confessed, "but if they did, what could have stopped them?"

"A government," Gar said. "I think the government collapsed

when the world from which your ancestors came stopped sending them food, medicine, and weapons."

"Do you really think sages could have stopped that?" Blaize asked.

"No," Gar said, "though it would have been awfully nice if they could have. But they could become a counterforce to the power of the magicians. The example of the sages might make the lords treat their serfs more gently."

"Perhaps," Blaize said doubtfully, "but most of the magicians I've heard of don't care that much for what anybody else thinks of them. Your sages would have to find a way of forming the people into little armies, to be able to fight off the wizards' guards—and how could they fight the lords' magic? Unless your sages were magicians themselves—but you tell me they don't believe in fighting."

"They don't," Gar confirmed, "but they also don't mind if a bully hurts himself when he's trying to hurt you."

Blaize gazed at him, knowing he was hearing a riddle. His mind circled the problem, nibbling at it. Then he straightened in surprise. "They found a way to make soldiers hurt themselves!"

Gar nodded. "Ways to make the soldiers' own blows work against them."

"What magic is that?"

"No magic, only a system of fighting," Gar assured him. "We'll teach it to you, but the basis of it is this: you become the rock over which your enemy trips."

It was an exciting idea, but Blaize had to wait to learn the philosophy first, and since Gar and Alea seemed to be learning it themselves, it would be a long wait. He filled the time as best he could with camp chores: hunting up a cave for their dwelling, sweeping it out, lashing branches together to make screens that divided the women's sleeping area from the men's and both from the living area. Mira helped, of course, but would only answer his questions with terse comments. That saddened Blaize, for chores could fill just so much of the day, and conversation would have lightened the rest—but Mira wouldn't talk with him any more than she absolutely had to. In fact, she seemed not just to despise him, but even to be afraid of him. That wounded Blaize. After all, he had done nothing to hurt her.

Finally he couldn't stand it any longer. One day, when he was carrying a basket of tubers he had dug back to camp, he met her as she was hauling a bucket of water from the stream. He fell in beside her and demanded, "Why do you despise me, Mira? I haven't hurt you in any way. I've given you no reason to be afraid of me."

"But you're a magician, even if you're not a very good one yet," Mira said, "and my magician lord summoned me to his bed. I'd seen what he'd done to other girls, so I ran away. He sent guards to chase me with dogs, then ghosts to scare me back toward the guards, and they would have caught me and hauled me back to his cruelty if Gar and Alea hadn't come along."

"A horrible man indeed." Blaize's face reddened. "He is a man corrupted by his own power—but then, that's all he really wants from life, isn't t? Power. For him, the pleasure of a beautiful woman is summoning her and knowing she doesn't dare refuse. His cruelty gives him pleasure only because it proves his power."

Mira looked at him in surprise. He seemed genuinely angry about Roketh.

"Most of them are like that, I'm afraid." Blaize looked as though he'd bitten into a rotten apple. "Corrupt, tyrannical, and cruel. I'd like to see every one of them hauled off his seat of power and chained in the bowels of the earth with enchanted manacles that would resist every spell. But there are a few good lords: Obiel of Lomark, Bockel of Hightree, and Erkin of Horgan, among others. They live modestly—or as modestly as you can in a mansion—and make sure their serfs have enough to eat and stout clothes to wear. But they have to be strong, very strong, for the others assume that a good man is a weak man and attack with all their powers, trying to swallow them up."

"There is no end to their greed!"

"No, there isn't—but there's another reason." Blaize turned to look out over the valley. "Word of a good magician gets out, you see, and makes other serfs begin to wonder if they can rid themselves of their cruel lords. Worse, the good lord's farmers grow more grain and fruit than those of the cruel lords—no wonder, since they're not weak from starvation."

"So the tyrants are jealous as well as greedy!"

"So jealous that you wonder their very hair doesn't turn green," Blaize agreed. "My own teacher Arnogle was a very good man. He was out among his serfs every day, making sure they were well fed and content with their lot, and if one wasn't, he sat down with that man or woman and asked why. If they thought they'd been treated unjustly, he brought in their hetmen and thrashed the problem out, even if it meant trying to cure a bad marriage. If someone was sick, he did all he could—not enough, alas, for he wasn't a healer. If one of them died, he'd be glum about it for days. And he never took a serf woman to his bed, even if it were her idea—said he'd had enough of that when he was young and had seen the unhappiness it could bring."

Mira turned wary again. "How many women had he despoiled in his youth?"

"None," Blaize said with certainty. "He told me he had never forced a woman, nor even pressed her to give him her favors, but there were four over the years who did press *him*, and you can't be surprised if he accepted."

"But he never married one of them?"

"No. He was homely, you see. Two had expected advantages from him—not be to have to work in any way, and to be able to lord it over the other women. One other expected fine clothes and jewelry, but he didn't take such things for himself—he thought the money was better used for repairing the serfs' cottages—"

"They had cottages? Not hovels?" Mira asked in surprise.

"Oh, yes, good thatched cottages—he set the men to building whenever there was no work to do in the fields. He thought the woman who asked for such luxuries was robbing her fellows, and became saddened. The fourth, as it happened, was more interested in stirring up jealousy in a lover who had turned from her to another woman. She succeeded well enough, and when the handsome young man came storming back to her, she left Arnogle on the instant."

Mira blinked. "But he was their lord! Didn't he punish them?"

"What for? A few nights of delight? For being in love? No, Arnogle wasn't that sort of man. He was saddened, though, and never dallied with a woman again. This was all before I joined him, of course," Blaize added. "He didn't tell me himself—I heard it piecemeal from the guards and the serfs."

"I didn't know there were such lords," Mira said, wide-eyed.

"There are a few, and I want to be like him in every way—except, of course, strong enough to fight off the neighbors who try to conquer my estates," Blaize amended. "And I'd like to succeed in love, but I've seen what happens to ugly men."

Mira almost blurted out that he was anything but ugly, but caught herself in time. Instead she summoned some indignation. "You mean to accept women's invitations, then? Don't worry, I won't give one. You can turn elsewhere with your lust."

"But with you, it isn't lust," Blaize said, wide-eyed and open-faced. "It's love."

Something seemed to melt within Mira—but something else shrieked with alarm. Shaken, she said, "Magicians can't love. Everyone knows that. Look elsewhere still, sir." She turned away, walking quickly back toward Gar and Alea, hurrying so fast that the water slopped over the brim of the bucket.

Blaize gazed mournfully after her. He should have known not to tell a woman he loved her before she'd come to know him well. Whatever ground he'd gained with her, he'd just lost.

She didn't seem to despise him quite so much anymore, though. That was something. At least she seemed uncertain. She might not think Blaize was a paragon of virtue, but at least she was no longer sure he was a villain. He'd have to settle for that.

The cave Blaize had found for their campsite was a gap in a cliff face that backed a broad ledge overlooking a valley. The ledge was fifty feet deep, so they had to go fairly close to the edge to look down on the villages below. There were half a dozen, most clearly seen in morning and evening, when their cookfires rose from the patchwork fields below.

Gar insisted they use green wood for their own campfire. He wanted plenty of smoke so the villagers below would notice. Mira and Blaize dutifully scooted around the fire whenever the wind changed, trying to cook food that wouldn't smell like pine or spruce.

When they weren't chopping wood or hauling water, though, they took lessons from Alea or Gar, whichever one wasn't meditating at that moment. The two of them taught the younger people the *Tao Te Ching*, of course, reading it to them— but they also insisted Mira and Blaize learn to read it for themselves. Reading led to writing, and before they knew it, Mira and Blaize were actually putting the sounds of the letters together to make words, and words to make sentences—slowly at first, haltingly, but writing.

Blaize looked up at Alea in awe. "Why didn't Arnogle teach me this?"

"Perhaps he didn't know it himself," she answered. "Was the magic he taught you written in books?"

"No, he told me about it and coached me in trying it." Blaize frowned. "But it should have been written down—at least the part of it that you don't have to feel for yourself."

"Maybe you can explain what it feels like," Alea suggested.

"Maybe I can." Blaize picked up his pen and began to write.

Mira looked on, wondering if she was watching the writing of the first book of magic and wondering also how she felt about that.

The two wanderers also taught Blaize and Mira to meditate. "You can't just read about the Tao," Gar explained. "You have to experience it." He sat cross-legged before them, teaching them to slow their breathing, to let their emotions smooth out and their thoughts calm and fade so that they could really begin to sense the world around them and feel for the Tao, the harmony of wind and tree, earth and fire.

Still, there were chores to be done. "You'll have to do the scutwork," Gar told the younger duo. "The peasants are growing so curious that they'll begin to sneak up and spy on us, and they won't believe Alea and I are sages if they see us scouring pots."

"The lot of apprentices everywhere," Blaize told Mira with a sigh. "Well, I'm used to it."

"I'm used to it, too," Mira answered, "and I wasn't even an apprentice!" She wondered how Gar knew the villagers were growing curious, then remembered that he could hear thoughts. She was glad she hadn't asked.

She did ask Alea if there were any reasons for herself and Blaize to be doing chores, other than putting on a show. Alea told her, and when the work became too boring, Mira told it to Blaize as a way of starting a safe conversation.

"Alea says we have to do the gathering and cooking and cleaning so that we can learn humility, patience, and obedience to the order of things."

"I've already learned plenty of humility, thank you." Blaize grunted as he swung one end of a log into place to make a seat by the fire, "and if an apprentice in magic doesn't understand the importance of obedience both to his master and to the laws of magic, I'd like to know who does." He picked up the other end of the log.

Mira set her hands on her hips. "There you go, trying to lord it over me because you've had some learning."

"Lord it over you?" Blaize looked up in astonishment—and dropped the log. "Ow! Oh-oh-oh-oh! My toe!"

"Is it badly hurt? Here, let me see!" Mira pushed him backward to sit on the log and reached for his foot.

"No, no! Just a bruise, I'm sure, nothing more!" But Blaize cradled the injured member in his other hand. "Believe me, I'm not telling you anything about how much you have to learn— only that even in the earliest days of my apprenticeship, I may have spent the day sweeping up and hauling water, but Arnogle always found a few minutes every day to teach me a little about magic."

"Well, so do Gar and Alea," Mira countered. "In fact, they're teaching us almost as quickly as they learn it themselves. Here, are you sure that toe isn't mashed?"

"Believe me, if it were, I'd know it," Blaize protested.

"You're just trying to act bravely!"

"Well, of course," Blaize said in surprise. "If it were really hurt, though, I'd be brave about the pain while I tied it in a splint." He set his foot down and leaned on it experimentally.

"Ow! Not just yet—which is what Gar says about teaching me magic."

"Well, we've only just begun to learn to meditate," Mira said practically. "Alea told us we needed to learn the Tao before we learned magic."

"Why?" Blaize grumbled. "I'm not learning any magic by meditating. Besides, they're just learning about the Tao now, and they've both known magic for years. I think Gar even grew up with it."

Mira frowned. "What makes you say that?"

"His trying to read his little brother's mind across an ocean of stars. That sounds like magic to me, and if two brothers know it, their parents would have, too, wouldn't they? So they learned it the way we learned reaping and mowing—helping as little children, tying sheaves as big boys and girls, then mowing when we were full grown."

Mira started a retort, then hesitated. "There might be something to that. . . ."

"Doesn't matter if there is," Blaize said with a sigh. He pushed himself upright, carefully putting a little weight, then a little more, on his injured toe. "It hurts, but it works."

"If it starts hurting worse, you sit down on the instant," Mira said sternly.

He looked up, beaming at her so warmly that she shrank away a little. "I will," he said softly, "and thank you."

Mira didn't ask for what. She did talk to Alea, though, as soon as she could catch her alone, when the two of them went to the stream to gather rushes. "Blaize is growing discontented."

"Really?" Alea looked up. "Why?"

"Well, we've been fetching and carrying for three weeks now, and you're teaching us how to meditate, but Blaize thinks you're never going to teach us your magic."

"We don't really know enough about his kind of magic to add to it," Alea said slowly, "but I suppose we'll have to learn."

She must have told Gar, because that very evening, when dinner was done and the dishes cleaned and put away, Gar sat Blaize down by the fire and said, "time to take the first small step toward magic, Blaize."

"Really?" the young man asked eagerly. "What do I do?"

"Put yourself into a light trance—you know how to do that now. You, too, Mira. Come sit with us and meditate."

Slowly and with misgivings, Mira sat cross-legged in front of him, smoothing her skirt down over her knees, then setting her palms on her thighs and straightening her back. Alea sat beside her and touched her hand for reassurance. Mira darted a look of gratitude toward her, then turned back to Gar and closed her eyes.

She pictured a blank gray wall, let it fill her vision, then before she let the tiny black dot appear on its expanse, glanced at Blaize. He sat, eyes closed, face rapt, seeking. The sight both bothered and reassured her somehow, but she closed her eyes again and let the black dot appear in the blank gray wall, then let it expand, growing slowly but steadily as a dozen thoughts whirled through her head but, one by one, began to settle and drop away. She knew Blaize was doing the same, and the black circle was no doubt growing behind his own eyes, growing and growing as his thoughts calmed to leave his mind blank.

But the dot began to make a noise, a groan that grew louder and louder, and a swaying white shape appeared in the black circle. Mira shrieked and leaped up, opening her eyes. Alea's hand seized hers, and she needed it, because the white shape was still there, swaying in the darkness beyond the edge of the cliff, and there were others like it, darting and advancing from the cliff path and actually stepping out of the wall of rock.

"Um, Blaize," Alea said, "I think you had better open your eyes and look about you."

Blaize looked up blinking. His eyes widened as he saw the ghost. Then he heard the moans from his left, from his right, behind him. He turned to look, this way, that way, then back up at Gar, beaming. "It works! Never before have I summoned so many!"

8

L et's hope your bargaining works better, too," Gar said nervously. "Talk to them, Blaize."

"Talk?" Blaize looked up at the ghosts, some formless and faceless, most looking exactly like people, some grim, some amused, some with wicked grins. "What would you have me say to them?"

"That we're friends, for starters." Gar swallowed, his eyes bulging. "That we're sorry to bother them, and they might as well go back to sleep."

"Ghosts don't sleep," Blaize said, not really thinking about it. "They would be cross indeed if they felt we had summoned them to no purpose, Master."

"I'm not your master!"

"Teacher, then. Can we not find some question to ask them?"

Gar's eyes began to glow; he seemed to relax a bit. "Yes, now that you mention it. There might be one or two things we'd like to know."

"How would you have me speak to them?"

Gar pursed his lips, thinking fast. "Well, you might begin with hello."

"Not courtly enough." Blaize shook his head, then raised his voice. "Good evening, O Ancestors of Our Kind. We greet you and honor you."

"Courteous, at least," rumbled a frowning ghost with jowls, a large nose, and a fringe of hair around a bald pate. "If you have summoned us to no purpose, you shall regret it sorely!"

Gar eyed the specter's clothing, trying to place it—a sort of open-necked doublet with tight-fitting trousers; the clothing might almost have been a businessman's suit of several hundred years before, romanticized and made a bit more dashing.

"We have certainly not called upon you in vain," Blaize said quickly. "My teachers seek information which only ancestors can give. They are strangers in this country and seek to better the lot of the common people."

"The common people! Faugh!" the rotund ghost said. "I am the Sorcerer d'Autrois, and I know of my own serfs that their lot should not be bettered—they must be kept in their place!"

A scream of anger pierced the air and another ghost streaked toward the first, snapping to a halt and yelling into his face, nose to nose. He wore rough tunic and hose and was considerably younger than the sorcerer. "Never should they submit to your yoke, villain! Now after death you know the truth—that you, too, are common, or that all of us are noble!"

"One might almost say that death has made you all equal," Gar interjected.

"Be still, foolish human!" the sorcerer thundered.

"No, speak, for you pronounce good sense!" The serf turned, bending down toward Gar. "Equal in death we are indeed, for what little magic one ghost can do, any other ghost can do, too! Fools that we were, not to see that we were equal in life, too."

"You were never my equal in life!" the sorcerer bellowed. "You had not a tenth of my power, not a hundredth!"

"No, but we were a thousand to your one!" The serf turned on him again. "If we had ceased to fear death and marched on you together, you would not have had a tenth of *our* power, and we would have hauled you out of your mansion to your death!"

"Spoken like the craven knave you are! You would never have dared death, for you knew the ghosts would eat your soul!"

"Yes, you made us tremble with that lie," the serf said with a nasty smile, "but we all know the truth of it now, don't we?"

"I do not!" Blaize cried. "Tell me, tell!"

"Do not!" the sorcerer ordered. "You know that is forbidden to the living!"

"Forbidden by whom?" the serf sneered, and turned to Blaize. "Know that it is not the ghost who devours the human's soul, lad, but—"

With a roar of anger, the sorcerer's ghost plunged into the serf's. Shouting and screaming filled the clearing as the amorphous glowing blob that was the two together heaved and twisted and bulged.

"Stop that now! Stop!" shouted another voice, and a fourth echoed it, "Stop!"

Two ghosts plunged into the melee from either side, actually into the glowing cloud itself, doubling its size. The amorphous form pinched in the center, its two halves drawing apart and settling into the forms of serf and sorcerer again, glaring at each other and spitting insults—but in front of each and blocking it from its enemy was a ghost in hooded tunic and hose, a bow and quiver on his back, a dagger at his belt, each firmly forbidding its prisoner to fight.

"Really, now!" said the sorcerer's restrainer, "you're setting a horrible example for our descendants!"

"No descendants of mine, you common fool!" roared the sorcerer.

"Come now, cousin, we're all common here," the guard said. "Aren't we, Conn?"

"All equal in death," Conn agreed, and gave the sorcerer a wolfish grin. "Shall I shoot an arrow into you to prove it?"

The sorcerer shuddered but still tried to bluster. "You are common fellows—woods runners!"

"Outlaws we are." Ranulf shrugged. "For me, it was the greenwood or the ruined city with its madmen and twisted outcasts. I chose the forest."

"City lunatic or forest outlaw, it's all the same!" the sorcerer spat. "You're bandits and should be hauled to the gallows!"

"Why, so I was," Conn told him, "and if you had been the lord who ordered it, I would make a pincushion of you, then follow as you recovered and pull out my darts, the better to fill you with them again. Ranulf, now, there was no gallows for him. A keeper sprang from ambush and put a sword through his heart, didn't he, Ranulf?"

"That he did," the other outlaw answered, "but I bear him no ill will for it. After all, I had laid an ambush for him the day before."

Blaize stared, his face tragic. "I had thought there was peace in the grave!"

"Oh, there is," Conn told him, "but we're not exactly in our graves, are we?"

"I'm sure our souls are peaceful," Ranulf said, "filled with bliss and delighting in the glory due those who were downtrodden during life—but we aren't those souls, only shadows of minds."

"Be still, you fool!" the sorcerer shouted.

"Fool?" Conn asked. "Well, I was a fool once—a jester until

my magician lord ordered my true love to his bed. I came to amuse him as he disrobed and drew a dagger from my bauble to plunge into his heart. Then I ran to the greenwood with my lass, but his ghost followed and learned by accident what happened when he ran upon a sword made of cold steel." Conn shook his head, remembering. "It blasted my arm to a lifeless lump for a day and more."

"Grounding out electrical charges?" Gar said, eye gleaming. "Very interesting."

"Electrical?" Another ghost shot forward to hover over Gar. "What manner of man are you who knows of electricity?"

Gar looked the phantom up and down. It wore a tall pointed hat and long robe; even in the pale glowing cream color of its substance, he could make out stars and moons and signs of the zodiac. "What manner of man should know it? A magician."

"Throw a fireball, if you are," the ghost challenged.

Blaize turned to Gar with a sinking stomach. "Don't tell them you are a fire-caster!"

"Am I?" Gar asked mildly. He gazed off into the night for a minute, then causally raised his hand and swung it toward the ghost. As his hand arced downward, fire seemed to gather in his palm, then spring off his fingertips straight toward the spectral magician. The phantom shrieked and disappeared. The fireball shot onward; the ghosts screamed and leaped aside from it. It struck against the face of the cliff in a shower of sparks and vanished.

"Yes, I suppose that's part of what I am," Gar conceded.

Blaize looked up at him, shaken. "Is there anything you can't do?"

"Quite a bit," Gar said. "Just ask Alea."

"No, we'll ask you instead." Conn floated away from his serf and glowered down at Gar. "The lad says he called us here at your request. What do you want of us?"

"Yes, what?" Ranulf drifted over, too. "Ask!"

"Well enough, then," Gar said, unruffled. "What are you made of?"

Several ghosts gasped in shock and several muttered about rudeness, but Conn only grinned. "What are *you* made of, mortal? If you can tell us that, maybe we can tell you our substance."

"A bargain," Gar said. "I'm made of protoplasm, mostly in the form of muscle, blood, bone, and sinew. And you?"

Conn lost his grin. "Like that, is it? Well, we're made of ectoplasm, my lad—ectoplasm, and a fine stuff it is."

"Fine indeed," Gar agreed. "What is it?"

The ghosts were all silent for a minute, glancing from one to another, clearly nonplussed. Then the sorcerer blustered, "It's not for a mere mortal to know what ectoplasm is!"

An order from him was all the incentive Conn needed. "Not for us to know, either," he said with a roguish smile. "It's a mortal word, don't you know—one our ancestors brought from the stars, if the old legend is true, and I've met some ghosts who swear it is, because they claim they came from old Terror herself—or so they say. If it was anything like they tell it, a terror it was, and no wonder they wanted to leave it."

"Terra it is, and a wonder in its own way," Gar answered. "Still, there must be something you can tell me about the way your substance behaves."

The ghosts exchanged glances. "Well, now," said the serf, "why would we be telling it to a ghost-leader like your lad here?"

"Why not?" Gar countered. "If you know he can already lead you, there's no danger in letting me know more about you. Besides, I've already learned how to cancel you with Cold Iron— or any sort of metal, I suspect."

Blaize glanced at him with keen interest. He'd have to persuade Gar to explain it to him later. It could be very handy, having some kind of threat to hold over a ghost's head.

"There's some truth in that," Conn admitted.

"Aye, some," Ranulf agreed.

"Don't you dare!" roared the old sorcerer. "You don't know what use he would make of the knowledge!"

Conn's grin hardened as he gazed at the shadow of power. "Your time for giving orders is past, old man." He turned back to Gar. "All we know is that if the weather becomes very, very cold, we turn into water, my lad—water, but we know it and still hold our shape and our thoughts within it."

"Fool!" ranted the old sorcerer. "Don't you see how he can use this against you?"

"Frankly, no," said Conn, "but I can see him drowning if he tries."

"Or freezing," Ranulf chimed in. "How would you rather die, mortal? Drowning or freezing?"

"Neither is really my favored mode of departing this earth," Gar answered. "So you're still aware of being yourselves even if you become fluid ghosts, are you? And still able to think?"

"Better and more clearly than ever," the old sorcerer snapped, "so if you think we poor ghosts can't work magic, don't come near us then!"

"Cold Iron probably wouldn't do much to you in that phase-state," Gar agreed, "though you might do something to it. How about your forms at normal temperatures? I notice you're all bigger than we are by half."

"Well, we don't have to be, that's true," the old serf admitted, grinning, "but we rather like looking down on our descendants."

"And you can't come out by day?"

"Try to get away from us after sunrise and find out," the old sorcerer boasted. "You just can't see us because the sun is brighter than we are, that's all."

"But you're still there." Gar nodded. "You're phosphorescent, though, so you glow as soon as it's dark enough—and the darker the night, the brighter the ghost."

"We only look that way," Conn confided. "We really stay the same brightness all the time."

"Of course, some of us are brighter than others," the old sorcerer said spitefully.

"No need to be jealous, old thing," Ranulf said easily.

"Even a peasant can outshine you now, if he's halfway virtuous," the old serf jeered.

The old sorcerer swelled up sputtering.

"How is it you can appear from thin air, then?" Gar asked.

"Oh, we can stretch our substance out so thin that mortals can't see it even at night," Ranulf answered.

Blaize stared. "You mean you're there already, but we can't see you?"

"Right you are, lad," Conn said. "Always there. Hundreds of us, thousands of us all about you, all the time. You'll never know when we're watching."

Blaize glanced at Mira, then looked away.

"Well, not all the time," Ranulf qualified. "Sometimes there isn't a ghost for miles around."

"Don't tell him that!" the younger magician snapped.

"I will if I choose," Ranulf said easily. "Point is, though, lad, you can't know, can you?"

"An ever-present threat," Mira quavered.

"No, not really." Alea stared up at the old sorcerer narrow-eyed. "Not the threat part, anyway. After all, some of us have old scores to settle, and I doubt even an old roué like that one could match our anger."

"Don't be so sure," the sorcerer blustered.

"Hell hath no fury like a woman scorned, you old fool." A bent, gnarled woman shouldered through the sorcerer—literally.

He gave a cry of distress. "Don't do that! You know how that makes me feel!"

"Aye, and I know how you made me feel while I was alive," the old woman snapped, "or one much like you." She turned to Alea and Mira. "Sorcerers, magicians—what's the difference? They're all alike. Alive or dead, all that changes is how much they can hurt you."

"You might be surprised!" the old sorcerer threatened.

"If I could be, you would have surprised me long ago," the hag returned. "No, I can cause you as much distress and shame as you can cause me, now—and for a very long time, too!"

"A long time?" Blaize asked. "You mean you don't last for eternity?"

The ghosts fell quiet, glancing at one another, clearly uncomfortable. Then the hag turned to Blaize again. "There isn't a one of us has just fallen apart and faded away, young fellow, though one or two have met with some very nasty accidents."

"Don't tell him that!" the magician snapped.

"Too late," Gar said mildly. "We already know about Cold Iron—and I can imagine what lightning would do."

The magician gave him a look that should have turned him into a ghost on the spot.

Alea glared at him, eyes fiery, and the old magician shrieked and clutched his head. "Stop! Make her stop!"

"No need for that just yet, my shield," Gar said softly. "After all, he can't tell us much with a tearing headache, can he?"

Alea relaxed to a simmer.

"I won't tell you anything ever!" the sorcerer blustered.

"You already have," Gar reminded him. "You just hadn't meant to."

"Indeed? What, for example?" the sorcerer demanded.

"That you're extremely long-lived," Gar said. "I'd guess that comes from having very little mass to keep up—though how you replenish yourselves I haven't figured out yet."

"From people's spirits," Mira quavered.

"If they did that, they wouldn't be completely themselves anymore," Gar pointed out. "I don't think any of them wants to risk a guest in the head."

The magician grinned. "You just keep thinking that way, lad."

"I don't think you can draw on people's life energy, either," Gar mused, "since we're Terran, and you're made of the substance of this planet."

"You might be surprised."

"I try to expect the unexpected," Gar told him. "Of course, the appeal of human life force might be why you appear when Blaize, or any other ghost-leader, summons you."

"Yes it might, mightn't it?" the sorcerer said, gloating.

"On the other hand, it might not," Conn said, giving the sorcerer a dark look.

"Of course," said the hag, "it *could* be simply that we like the feel of human thoughts—but we wouldn't talk about that, now, would we?"

"Then don't," the sorcerer snapped.

"Why not?" Alea grinned.

Gar nodded. "You're creatures of thought, mostly, so human thoughts might wake agreeable sensations in you."

"They warm themselves at our fires!" Alea exclaimed. "You come crowding to feel our emotions, don't you?"

"Anger, love, hatred, sympathy, grief, gratitude—no wonder you cluster around deathbeds," Gar mused. "Tell me, what does lust feel like to a ghost?"

"Delightful," the old sorcerer sneered.

"Don't pretend you can still feel it, you old idiot." The crone sniffed. She turned to Alea. "They're as different as flavors of food are to you, child. Love doesn't feel like the love I remember, but it wakens a delicious sensation in me, one I can't find words for. So do pity and desire and contentment—"

"And fear," the sorcerer interrupted, grinning. "Fear feels best of all, a thrill and a glow and elation."

"That's why you try to frighten us!" Blaize cried. "That's why you haunt!"

"Those who haunt, yes." The crone threw the sorcerer a look of disgust. "Those who haunt and don't have a good reason, such as crying for justice or warning of danger. Yes, ghosts like him delight in human fear and pain."

"The emotions become compelling, do they?" Gar asked, somewhat detached and clinical.

"I hunger for them," the sorcerer said, grinning, and some of the other ghosts chorused agreement, magicians, hulking bandits, old roués still handsome in age forever fixed, and sly evil-looking courtiers.

"Compelling, yes," Gar said thoughtfully. "I might even say addictive. So if a mind reader directs anger against you, the feeling is too intense. What would happen if you didn't flee from it? Would it shake you apart?"

"You've no need to know that, foolish mortal," the sorcerer bellowed.

"You're right, of course," Blaize said to Gar, though his gaze was still on the ghosts. "I *am* learning a deal of magic tonight."

"Not least is that you are apparently a projective empath, and a powerful one," Gar said. "That means you feel what others feel and send out your own feelings to waken them in others. That's why the ghosts come flocking whenever you summon them—because you send out emotion, whatever emotion you're feeling at the time, whether it be fear or curiosity or joy. They come soaring to taste."

"Would you really flee if I felt anger at you?" Blaize asked.

"You? Not likely," the sorcerer said scornfully.

"It's a matter of strength, boy," Conn explained. "That woman with you, now, she's been hurt sometime in her life and hurt badly, and it's left her with a river of fury likely to spill over its banks at the slightest insult. When she feels anger, it cuts like a whiplash. You, lad, if you want feelings that will do us any harm, think about folk who have wronged you or wronged people you love, then aim it at whatever ghost you want to shake apart."

"Traitor," the sorcerer hissed.

"I never swore allegiance to you or your kind," the outlaw retorted, "and I never asked to become a ghost."

"Something in you did," the magician snapped, "or you'd never have twisted a wild spirit to your likeness."

"You mean if I can make my anger intense enough, I can scare ghosts away?" Blaize asked.

"Well, we wouldn't really go very far," Conn temporized, "just thin enough and far enough away so you couldn't see us."

"Aye," said Ranulf. "Then we'd coast along beside you, like a hunter stalking a stag, waiting for you to fall in love or taste a delicious meal or look out at a beautiful sunrise."

"Or lust after a beautiful woman," the crone snapped, glaring at the magician.

"That's why ghosts come so quickly to me?" Blaize asked. "Because you can tell I'm going to be feeling deeply?"

The ghosts fell silent, glancing at one another.

"You've guessed rightly," Alea said. "The more mental energy a person gives off, the more these creatures are attracted to that person—and as Gar said, you're an empath, unusually talented."

"Perhaps also gifted with an unusual sensitivity. What you feel, you feel very sharply and deeply."

Mira's gaze snapped to Blaize, but the boy only said, "Do I?"

"You do make quite a racket, when you're calling for help or even just company," Ranulf admitted.

"Not one word more! Not one!" the sorcerer thundered, fists on hips. "He is our quarry, not we his!"

"Congratulations," Gar told Blaize. "You're a natural resource."

"Don't you mean a *super* natural resource?" the magician sneered.

"No, that's you—or the stuff you're made of, anyway." Gar looked up, spectacularly unintimidated, at the ghost who towered over him. "You do know, of course, that people with his talent are rare."

"Of course we know that!" the magician said contemptuously.

"If they were not," the sorcerer said with scathing scorn, "how would they gain power among their fellow humans?"

"In the usual ways," Gar said easily. "Power is power, and its abuse is an old story."

The sorcerer huffed up and the magician's eyes narrowed, but the crone cackled.

"Such talent is even more rare, however, among the people of Terra, from whom your ancestors came," Gar said, "so rare that few people believe there really is such a thing. How did these gifts develop among your people?"

Silence fell over the ghosts; they looked from one to another, startled—the idea had never occurred to any of them before.

9

Finally Conn turned back to Gar. "No one here knows, mortal."

Gar stared at him for a moment. Alea watched, frowning, wondering what he was thinking, then realized what it must have been: the ghosts had obviously conferred with one another, but in a way she and Gar couldn't hear—telepathy on a different set of frequencies, perhaps? Or in a different mode?

Gar said, "None of you here? But there are some who do, many miles away?"

"There are," the crone said, eyeing him warily.

"Tell him nothing more than he needs to know!" the sorcerer barked.

"Why not?" Gar asked. "After all, your ghost-leaders have already discovered this for themselves." He looked up at Conn. "Would you do me the courtesy of getting in touch with one of those first ancestral ghosts and asking him my question?"

"Not for a second!" the sorcerer snapped.

Conn gave him a glance of annoyance. "To spite you, I

might." He turned back to Gar. "It's not so easily done, fellow. I can't talk to one so distant mind to mind, after all."

"Not one so distant?" Gar looked thoughtful. "There's potential there."

Conn frowned. "What do you mean?"

"Nothing that we can do right now," Gar said. "It would take a great deal of thought and planning, then a string of very boring experiments—and I gather you have all had your fill of boredom."

The ghosts gave a start of surprise; then the magician said warily, "What makes you say a thing like that?"

"Why else would you be so eager to flock to a person like Blaize, whose feelings overflow for you to sense?"

"Don't answer that," the magician snapped.

"I'll answer what I please," Conn snapped back. "When will you shadows of power learn that you have no authority past the grave?" He turned back to Gar. "I might be interested in these experiments you speak of, mortal—at first that is. If they become boring, of course, that would be another matter."

"Could you find me someone to take up where you left off?" Gar asked.

Conn exchanged a glance with Ranulf. "Yes, that should be possible."

"Let me work it out," Gar said. "I'll let you know as soon as I'm ready to try it."

"Try what?" the sorcerer asked suspiciously.

"A sort of message relay, like couriers on horseback."

"We're not your servants!"

"I never said you were," Gar said easily, "but if some of you choose to relieve your boredom by testing an idea, I won't turn your courtesy away."

The magician fixed him with a gimlet glare. "You are far too glib, mortal."

"Yes, I know what you mean," Gar sighed. "Sometimes I don't even trust myself. But I'll let you know when my divertissement is ready, and you can judge my worthiness then."

"I know it now," the sorcerer said.

"But I don't." Conn grinned. "Let me know when you're ready to begin, Magician."

"Maybe then." Ranulf yawned elaborately. "For myself, I find this exchange is growing dull. Good night, mortals, and may good fortune speed your amusements." He flickered like a candle in a draft and disappeared.

The yawn was contagious; several of the other ghosts shared it, then began to wink out, one by one, until only the sorcerer, the magician, and Conn were left.

"They haven't really gone, have they?" Gar asked.

"Most of them, yes," Conn said. "Your novelty has worn off."

"But some of them arc still around?"

"I will always be near." The sorcerer made his tone a threat.

"Well, then, so will I." Conn locked gazes with the tyrant's shade and grinned.

"Fear ghosts," the magician intoned, glaring at Alea, Mira, and Blaize. "Fear our power!"

"But you have no power over the living," Blaize objected, "as long as we refuse to be frightened."

"Are you truly so courageous as that?" The ghost floated closer, growing, towering over Blaize, swollen and threatening.

"Yes, he is," Conn said, "especially since he knows I'm here to boggle you if you become too much of a nuisance."

"Be still, peasant!"

"Oh, really! You command me, do you?" Conn threw back his head and began to sing, loudly and off-key.

In Scarlet Town, where I was born,
There was a fair maid dwellin'—

The sorcerer winced. "Enough!"

"Not by half." Conn sang again.

Maybe ev'ry lad cry well-a-day,
Her name was—

"I can't take it anymore," the sorcerer groaned. "You've been warned, mortals!" He winked out.

Conn broke off and turned grinning to the companions. "Yes, be warned, but don't think you have anything to fear from the likes of him. Oh, he can make you feel fear even if he can't really scare you, but that's all he can do."

"As long as we remember that all we have to fear is fear itself," Gar said, "he can't hurt us."

"Well said, well said." Conn nodded approvingly.

"It was a wiser man than I who first said it."

"And you're wiser than any magician I've met," Conn returned, "though I have heard of a few who realize that the good they do comes back to them—especially when they become ghosts. Well, be careful, mortals. We phantoms may not be able to hurt you, but living magicians and their guards can."

"What of forest outlaws?" Alea asked.

Conn bared his teeth in a grin. "They'll hear from me if they do!" He winked out.

The campsite was silent for a minute. Then Gar cleared his throat and said, "I think we can conclude that going into a trance helps summon ghosts."

"Yes, I would say that was clear," Alea said sarcastically.

"However, I'd prefer to leave the rest of the lesson until tomorrow." Gar rose and stretched. "If you don't mind, my friends, I'd just as soon lie down for the night. We'll work on spectral communications tomorrow, shall we?"

"Spectral communications?" Blaize frowned. "What's that?"

"Gossiping ghosts," Gar said. "Good night."

The next morning, when chores were done, Gar and Alea sat down with Mira and Blaize to start experimenting.

"First," Gar said to Blaize, "see if you can contact Conn and Ranulf."

"By daylight?" Blaize asked in surprise.

"Of course. You heard Conn last night—the ghosts are still here even if we can't see them. It's just that the sun's too bright."

"That's true." Blaize turned thoughtful. "Of course, they might not be right here with us."

"They might not indeed. That's why I'd like you to call and see if they are."

Blaize nodded, then closed his eyes. A few minutes later, he opened them, looking shaken. "They're here."

"I told you we'd stay near," said a thin, faint voice.

They all started, recognizing it as Conn's.

"I've an idea I'd like to try," Gar said. "Would you mind helping us, Conn?"

"Depends on what it is. Say, mortal."

"I'd like to see if you can put words into the mind of a person who can't read thoughts."

"Interesting notion," the ghost said. "Where will I find one?

"Well," Gar said, "I was thinking of Mira here."

Mira shrank away in alarm.

"Yes, I thought you might," Conn said. "She can read minds, you know."

"No I can't!" Mira cried.

"It's a faint talent, lass, so faint you're not aware of it—but haven't you ever noticed that you have a hunch what someone else is going to do before they do it?"

"Well, yes, but . . . everybody does, don't they?"

"Not all," Conn said, "but she has a point, mortal. Most folk in this land have some little ability to read minds—very little, mostly, but it's there. It's one of the things you learn being a ghost."

"Well, then," Gar said, obviously digesting as he spoke, "would you mind waiting for Conn's words to come into your mind, Mira?"

"I . . . I . . ."

"There's no harm in it, lass." Alea laid a reassuring hand over Mira's. "From what he says, ghosts do it all the time anyway."

"That's true," said Ranulf's voice, "but only when we're feeling mischievous."

Alea looked askance in the direction of his voice. "How often are you not?"

"Only when we're bored."

"When are you not bored?"

"When we're being mischievous."

Conn cut in. "Was there anything in particular you wanted Mira to hear, mortal?"

Instead of answering, Gar frowned at Blaize, who looked startled, then gazed off into the distance.

Mira frowned too. "Because they both begin with the sound 'r,' of course. But wasn't he supposed to try to make the words come into my mind?"

"He was," Gar said, "but you only heard him speaking more loudly than he had been, didn't you?"

"That's right."

"He didn't speak aloud, lass," Alea said. "I was careful to listen with my ears, not my mind, and you were the only one who heard his words."

Mira looked startled. Then she began to look frightened.

"I thought the question at Blaize," Gar said, "and he thought it at Conn, who thought it at you."

Mira still looked frightened, but she asked bravely, "Was I right?"

"It's as good an answer as any," Gar said. "The man who thought up the riddle didn't tell us the answer, and for six hundred years people have been trying to figure out why a raven is like a writing desk." He looked toward the section of air that had generated Conn's voice. "Could we try again, only this time, have Conn tell the question to Ranulf, who will tell it to Mira?"

"You're just saying that because I was feeling left out," Ranulf's voice answered.

"No, I really do have a purpose," Gar assured him. "Will you help?"

"Of course! This is really interesting. Ask away, mortal."

"This time, think the answer to Alea," Gar said, "and let's see if she can relay it to Mira. Is that all right, Alea?"

"As Ranulf said, this is becoming interesting." Alea sat up a little straighter, smiling. "Ask away!"

Gar's brow knit. Blaize gazed off into space. After a few seconds, Alea looked surprised, then Mira did, too. "How can one hand alone make the sound of clapping?"

"It can't, of course," Gar said, "but pondering that point will clear your mind of all other random thoughts. Thank you, Conn and Ranulf—it seems ghosts can pass messages from one to another, and the last can deliver the words to a mortal."

"I should have thought that was rather plain," Conn's voice sniffed.

"It was, but I wanted to make sure," Gar said. "Do you suppose ghosts would be willing to pass such a message from one to another over miles of land?"

"There would likely be many willing," Ranulf's voice said, "if for nothing but to pass the time—and of course, if the message had strong emotions toning it, they'd be all the more willing."

"Exactly what are you trying to invent here?" Alea asked.

"A ghost-to-ghost hookup," Gar answered.

"It bothers me." Blaize did look agitated. "This is too much manipulation of spirits; it seems more like the way most of the ghost-leaders go about controlling the specters—by blackmail and bribery, not by the sort of persuasion my master Arnogle used."

"We heard of Arnogle," Ranulf said. "There were more spirits willing to help him than any other ghost-leader, simply because his projects were exciting, which meant they were willing to protect him, too, so that the projects could go on."

"Little good it did him!" Blaize said mournfully.

"Some mortals become so excited that they won't listen to advice," Ranulf sighed. "Remember that, young fellow. When you do make friends of a ghost, pay attention to what it tells you."

"I shall," Blaize said fervently. "But is binding phantoms to service as messengers a way of making friends?"

"I would not be binding them," Gar objected, "only asking them to join in if it pleased them."

"But so many ghosts all at once, all on one errand! Surely that is greedy!"

"Rather selfish of us, you mean?" Alea asked. "Well, I suppose it is, if the message were only for our benefit, but I know Gar well enough to say that he would have the good of all the serfs in mind."

"Communications can be very important when you're resisting a tyrant," Gar agreed, "but we're not simply saying that the ends justify the means."

Blaize frowned. "What?"

"That it's all right for us to hurt people or exploit them, as long as it's going to end by making all the serfs happier, for instance," Alea explained.

Mira leaned backward, eyeing Alea as if at the end of a long pole. "I would be very wary of such an idea!"

"Many people fall into it," Gar said. "Alea and I try to resist it, though."

Alea nodded. "But we don't think there's anything wrong with the means in this case. Any ghosts helping with Gar's message chain would be doing so of their own free will—we're not planning to threaten or blackmail anybody."

"Neither living nor dead," Gar agreed.

Blaize wondered why Mira was looking at him in so strange a way. "So you're not trying to gain power and wealth for yourselves, and you're not enslaving anybody or forcing them to work for you."

Gar nodded.

"I can see no wickedness in that. I can't say that of very many other magicians, though."

"Are you planning to be like those other magicians?" Alea challenged.

"No!" Blaize declared. "Anything but that!"

"Well said." Conn's voice was approving. "If you ever gain power, boy, remember what you've said here."

"If you don't," Ranulf's voice promised, "we'll remind you."

Blaize couldn't help shuddering at the thought of the form their "reminding" could take. "I'll remember!" Then his shoulders slumped. "But I'm not likely to gain much power. So much for my dreams of being a good master!"

"Perhaps it would be better to work to eliminate all masters," Gar suggested.

"As though we could!" Alea scoffed. "You saw yourself how well that worked on Brigante! All they had done was change masters!"

"Well, yes," Gar agreed, "but the Scarlet Company was certainly the mildest lord I've ever seen."

"If it was, why were the people so frightened at the thought of going against its orders?"

"I don't want people to be frightened of me," Blaize said glumly.

Conn's voice heaved a weary sigh. "If you have any power at all, lad, people will be afraid when they stop to think what you can do—and if you don't have power, you can't do good."

"But I can't do evil, either!"

"Which will it be, then?" Ranulf's voice challenged. "Too weak to do any good, or keeping a close watch on yourself to make sure you don't do any harm?"

Blaize lowered his gaze, scowling.

"You have to decide, lad," Conn said. "You can't do the one without doing the other."

"Well—if I must—I'll choose to do good," Blaize said, "and trust you to tell me if I'm doing harm." Then he looked up, astounded. "What am I saying? I'm not likely to have the power to do either!"

"Oh, yes, you are," Conn said, "for you're a magician, albeit one who still has a lot to learn."

"You're a ghost-leader," Ranulf reminded him, "and you've won two ghosts most thoroughly to your side."

"Won? No! It was Gar who won you over."

"No, lad," Conn's voice said kindly. "It was your own agonizing about trying to make sure you used your power wisely and well."

"If you really mean to help the serfs, though," Ranulf said, "you might start paying attention to them. There are two crouching behind that yew, and three more watching from the rock pile against the cliff face."

Surprised, Blaize started to turn toward the yew, but Alea said softly, "Don't look."

Blaize froze—and found himself staring at Mira, who had been turning to look at the rock pile, too. For a moment, all he could see was her face, her eyes . . .

Then Gar's voice broke the spell. "You have to be careful if you try to do the head carpenter's job."

"Yes," said Alea. "You might cut your thumb."

Gar nodded. "So telling a man to do the master carpenter's job is like asking a turtle to dinner."

"Not a good idea," Alea returned, "if they're serving turtle soup."

Blaize stared in consternation, then leaned over toward Mira and asked out of the corner of his mouth, "What are they talking about?"

"Riddles of the Way," she answered, low-voiced. "We've both heard them go on like this, but they always explained them before."

"You mean they're actually trying to confuse the serfs?"

"Confuse them, or make them curious," Mira answered.

Blaize nodded slowly. "They're succeeding. They've certainly confused me, and I'm curious as to what they mean."

"Probably nothing," Mira opined.

"The highest virtue is low as a valley," Gar said.

"Yes," Alea agreed, "and the purest seems to be soiled."

"Vast virtue never seems to be enough," Gar lamented.

"The virtue of strength seems weak," Alea said.

"When you get right down to it," Gar sighed, "reality is simple, but it keeps seeming to change."

"All virtues are gathered in the Way," Alea answered.

"Of course," Gar said, "since the Way includes everything that exists."

"Including people," Alea said. "The uncarved block of wood is best."

"Yes," Gar said, "but somebody cut it into a block."

They went on and on. Eventually Blaize, confused by conundrums and bored by hearing what he'd heard before disguised as riddles, rose and went to chop some wood of his own. Mira apparently decided it was a good idea, for she came to her feet, went to fetch water, and set a kettle on to boil—without any turtles.

Finally, dazed and inspired, the serfs slipped away. Alea and Gar kept on until they were well out of sight; then Alea said, "I think we impressed them."

Gar's eyes lost focus for a moment. Then he smiled at her. "We did. They'll be back tomorrow, even though they haven't the faintest idea what we were talking about."

"I'm not sure I do myself," Alea confessed.

"Nor I," Gar agreed, "but we managed to get across the basic concept of the Tao and people's proper place in it."

"So tomorrow we work on how they gain and lose that place?" Alea asked with a grin.

"A good strategy." Gar nodded. "We might mention why they should want to."

"All very interesting," Mira called from the campfire, "but the stew is ready."

Gar and Alea stared at one another, then burst out laughing.

The serfs came back the next day, still in hiding—only there were eight of them now. Gar and Alea batted paradoxes back and forth like tennis balls while Blaize and Mira demonstrated how to put yourself in harmony with the Way by doing the camp chores. By the forth day there were fifteen peasants, and the youngest ones were edging closer and closer to the limit of the yew bush and the rock pile, perilously close to being clearly visible.

"Shall we give them the final nudge?" Gar asked.

"Let's," Alea said with a mischievous grin.

10

A lea took up the pouches of colored sand they'd collected for the occasion.

Gar tied a string to two pegs, tapped one into the ground for a center, then inscribed a circle in the dirt with the other. Alea sprinkled yellow sand in a tadpole shape that occupied one half of the circle, swelling from nothing at its tail to a bulbous head. Then she sprinkled red sand in the other half, so that she had two tadpoles, nestled head to tail, making up a complete circle. She dropped a little red to make a tiny circle for the yellow tadpole's eye and used yellow sand for the red tadpole's eye.

"Yellow is masculine, red is feminine," Gar intoned.

"Each holds within it the seed of the other," Alea answered.

"The masculine element is hot, dry, mechanical, and active.

"The feminine element," said Alea, "is cool, moist, organic, and passive."

Gar put a finger beside the edge of the circle at the midpoint of the yellow tadpole, which was also the midpoint of the red. "When both are in balance, the world is peaceful and prosperous."

The youngest serfs began edging out of hiding, craning their necks to see.

Gar traced a finger along the edge toward the yellow tadpole's head. "When the masculine element grows to take up most of the circle, though, governments are tyrannical. No one can think for themselves; everyone does what the king commands. There is always food, but the serfs are kept poor by high taxes."

The young folk crept closer. The older ones began to sneak out from cover.

Alea moved her finger to trace the red tadpole to its head. "When the feminine element takes up most of the circle, there is no government. Lords are constantly fighting one another, killing the serfs and trampling the crops, keeping people poor."

The young serfs crept closer, so intent on seeing the Great Monad that they didn't realize their shadows were falling across it.

"Only when there is balance are the people free, with the chance to find their own happiness," Gar said.

"Only when there is harmony can people be prosperous and safe," said Alea.

Mira came up behind one of the older serfs and said in a conspiratorial whisper, "You might as well sit down, you know. They love answering questions."

The serf jumped as though he'd just stepped on a live wire.

"You're all welcome here," Blaize told the people in the rock pile, "if you really want to learn. Oh, and when you're done, you might take a hand with the sweeping."

The serfs stared at him. Then, one by one, they came out from hiding. "Are—are you sure?" a middle-aged woman asked.

"Of course," Blaize said. "They've known you were there for days."

She stared in fright. "Are they . . . are they magicians?"

"Not as we usually think of them," Blaize said. "They're sages."

"Sit down," Alea invited one of the younger serfs, "and ask your questions."

The girl sat down at the side of the circle, warily, hesitantly. The boy beside her sat down, too, slowly. "How do you find harmony?" the girl asked.

"By putting yourself in balance," Alea answered.

A young man sat down on the other side of the circle, giving the impression of a rabbit about to bolt. "How do you find balance?"

"By seeking harmony with the Way," Gar replied.

A young woman sat down beside the young man, frowning. "What is this Way you keep talking about?"

Their elders came up behind them, wary but intent.

"The Way includes all things that exist," Alea explained. "Everything came from it; everything returns to it, as the rivers flow home to the sea."

"But the sea is never full," Gar said, "and the Way is empty."

"But it never needs filling," Alea said, "for everything is in it."

An older man frowned. "How can it be empty and full at the same time?"

"Because it is a paradox," Gar said, "an apparent contradiction."

"But only apparent," Alea reminded them. "It's like a puzzle, and there's always a way to solve it."

"How?" the man asked, totally bewildered.

"By experiencing the Way," Alea told him. "You can't really talk about it, for as soon as you do, as soon as you even give it a name, you limit it, and it isn't really the Way anymore—because the Way is limitless."

A girl asked, "So if I call it the Way, I've lost track of it?"

"Yes," Gar said, "but we have to call it something, and "way" is about as vague as we can get and still have a name."

"But as soon as you name it, it stops being what you named?" an older woman asked.

"That's right." Gar beamed at her. "Any name you can give it won't fit long, because it's always changing."

"But it's always the same, too," Alea put in, "because it's the source of everything."

"But I want to find out what it is!" the boy objected.

"Then you'll find what you expect to find," Gar told him, "but it won't be the real Way."

The older man frowned. "So we can only find it by not looking for it?"

"Exactly!" Alea clapped her hands with delight. "You have to wait until it finds *you.*"

"But how," the young woman asked, totally perplexed, "will we know when it does?"

"Believe me," said Alea, "you'll know."

The serfs left an hour later, confused but inspired.

"They won't come back, will they?" Mira asked mournfully.

"Are you joking?" Gar asked. "This is the most exciting thing that's happened to them in years!"

"Learning is always exciting." Blaize beamed, giving the impression that he was about to start bouncing. "I can hardly wait for tomorrow!"

Mira eyed him warily.

Gar decided to build a pavilion to shelter their students from the sun and rain, so he took Blaize downslope to hunt up some reasonably sized deadwood. Mira started making dinner, looking pensive.

"What's the matter, lass?" Alea asked gently.

Mira looked up, startled, then dropped her gaze again. "Oh, it's—it's nothing, Alea."

"Nothing named Blaize?" Alea smiled. "He bothers you, doesn't he?"

Reluctantly, Mira nodded.

"More doubts because he's a magician?"

"No, because he says he wants to be a good man as well as a good magician!" Mira looked up, eyes blazing. "Can he really mean it, Alea? Or was he just spinning a fable, putting on a show to make me think he's really trying?"

"Oh, he's sincere," Alea said. "You can feel the emotions leaking out of him. He means what he says."

"He could be pretending. . . ."

"If he is, he's very good at it, but even the best pretender can't fool a mind reader."

"Magicians can."

"Maybe an expert magician, one who specializes in mind reading—are there such?"

Mira nodded.

"But that's not Blaize's magic," Alea pointed out, "and even if it were, he's still an apprentice. No, he's an empath and he's learned how to project his emotions, but he hasn't learned how to hold them in."

"Is that why I feel as though I'm getting caught up by his enthusiasm?" Mira asked. "Caught up in his—" She broke off, blushing.

"Yes, he does have romantic moods, doesn't he?" Alea asked, amused. "He's still young enough so that they seem a little silly, don't they?"

"No!" Mira cried. "Hopeless and ill-placed, perhaps, and his ardor always seems to come at the wrong time, but I wouldn't call him silly!"

Alea gazed at her thoughtfully, then said, "It's real then, lass."

"What?" Mira asked in confusion. "His romantic notions or his desire to be good and still be a magician?"

"Both," Alea said, "but he'll need a lot of help. It's hard to gain power and not let it corrupt you."

Mira wondered if she were talking about magic or love. Then she began to wonder if there were any difference.

The villagers did come back the next day, but with several re-placements, and that was the pattern of it—never more than a dozen, but rarely did one person come more than two days in a row. Over the course of the month, Gar and Alea were sure they'd seen the entire adult population of the village.

"It's their lords," Mira explained, "and the guard who patrols the fields to watch over them. There's only one of him to fifty of them, so he's not going to notice if a few are gone any one day—in fact, if he does, he'll assume they're doing other work, such as gathering wood or mending walls or some such. But if it's the same few every day, he'll grow suspicious."

"So they come here in turns." Alea nodded. She didn't have to ask how Mira knew; it was a good guess that conditions were the same in her home village.

"We could let them come in the evenings," Blaize suggested.

"Don't be silly," Mira said. "They have to rise with the sun."

"Besides, the ghosts might put them off," Gar added.

That was certainly true. Blaize knew Conn and Ranulf were eavesdropping every day. He could feel their presence, and very often that of other ghosts whom he didn't know, too. In the evenings, the specters appeared to discuss the issues with Gar and Alea with enthusiasm and fascination. Several times argu-ments broke out between ghosts, and the living people began to realize that some of the ghosts were sages themselves. Finally Mira asked one of them, an old woman in a hooded robe, "Are you a magician?"

"Don't you dare call me that!" the old woman snapped. "Oh, I've seen our descendants take that title and start using the powers to intimidate people, but we didn't! Well, not most of us," she amended. "We were shamans, girl, and don't you forget it!"

"I won't," Mira promised, wide-eyed. "What is a shaman?"

The old woman sighed. "A sort of combination of priest, healer, counselor, teacher, and sage, young lady—all that, and more, even, yes, a little bit of a magician. We don't like that term, though. Our descendants have made it an obscenity by their corruption and cruelty."

"You're a wise woman!" A bit of Mira's fear of the supernatural came back—it was never far away.

"That does sort of wrap it all up, I suppose," the ghost said.

"Then should I call you Your Wisdom?"

"You should call me Elyena and nothing more!" the old woman snapped. "I might be your great-great-great-grandmother, but don't you dare call me that, either!"

Mira didn't think she could manage the string of "greats" everytime she wanted to talk to the old woman. "But—where did you gain your wisdom?"

"Why, from an older shaman, of course—several of them, in fact. But if you mean where did they get it, why! They took the ideas of the sages and philosophers of old Terra that our great-great-grandparents brought when they colonized this planet, and they mixed it with the discoveries they'd made themselves, generations of sages and gurus and priests. That's what it was by the time I learned it, lass: a wisdom and power that's peculiar to this world of Oldeira, and don't you forget it!"

"I won't." Mira shrank away, then plucked up her nerve and asked, "Is that why you don't like this talk of the Way?"

"Oh, Taoism's sound enough—at least the classical version before the Buddhists got hold of it," Elyena grumbled. "It's part of the foundation of Oldeira's wisdom—but only part, lass! And your friend's trying to make it seem something new, something that will supplant all the philosophy we've had such a time thrashing out and blending these past five hundred years."

"Maybe the serfs need to be reminded of it." Mira felt shockingly bold offering the idea. "Maybe that way the magicians will hear of it and realize they're doing something wrong."

"Stuff and nonsense!" Elyena snorted. "They know they're doing wrong and they don't care a whit! All they care about is wealth, power, and gaining all the luxuries and pleasures they can!"

"You—you think it's wrong of Gar and Alea to try to teach the Way, then?"

"Oh, it won't do any harm," the old woman said with a sniff, "but it won't do any good, either. You tell them I said that!"

Mira did. They thought it was very interesting, but they didn't stop teaching.

After the third week, though, Gar spent an evening sitting cross-legged staring out over the valley and came back to the campfire at bedtime looking very glum.

Mira saw the look of alarm on Alea's face but also saw how quickly she masked it even as she hurried to meet Gar, and for once there was no sarcastic turn to her words. "What's happened? What's the matter?"

"Oh, just the usual human cussedness." Gar tried to smile. "They're excited by our ideas, sure enough, and they're talking about them whenever they're sure the lord's men aren't listening—but they're grumbling and complaining about their lives as much as usual, bickering and taunting each other as much as they always did. The boys are still doing their best to seduce the girls, the girls are flaunting their bodies as much as they can in those clothes, and whenever people try to take a few minutes to meditate, their spouses accuse them of laziness."

"Don't be disheartened," Alea said with a tender smile. "They're only human. You can't expect them to change their ways overnight."

"No, I suppose not." Gar sat down by the campfire with a sigh. "Still, I'd hoped for some sign that they might actually start trying to live the Way instead of merely talking about it."

"Is there any sign that they're less bitter about the harshness of their lives?"

Gar was silent a moment, then said, "Now that you mention it, there is—a bit more acceptance, a little of the feeling that the life itself matters more than its comforts."

"Then they are listening," Alea said, touching his hand in reassurance. "They really are."

Mira wondered about the older woman's claim that Gar was only her friend—not even that, a traveling companion and shield-mate, which was both more and less. Did Alea really know her own heart?

Things weren't any better by the end of the fourth week, as far as Gar was concerned, but Conn told him, "We've been around and listening. They're beginning to see the lord's greed and cruelty not just as tyranny, but also as the result of being out of harmony with the Way."

"Are they really?" Gar asked, hope sparking in his eyes.

"They are," Ranulf assured him. "There's a sense growing in them that the lords are actually living wrongly."

"Could they ever have thought anything else?" Alea cried.

"Oh, yes," Mira said. "The lords are just part of the world, just the way things are."

Blaize nodded. "Rabbits are timid, wolves are ravenous, and lords are cruel. That's the way things have always been and the way they'll always be."

"And there's nothing you can do about it," Gar said grimly.

Blaize nodded. "You can suffer it, or you can die fighting back."

"And people are beginning to think of fighting back?" Alea asked.

"I haven't heard anything like that yet," Gar protested.

"You're right," Conn said, "but thinking the magicians are wrong is the first step toward thinking they're evil, and that means they're way out of harmony with the Way."

"Which means they should put themselves back in touch with it!" Gar slapped his knee in triumph. "The people are beginning to think the magicians should change!"

"That's how it begins," Alea said, glowing, "by thinking change is possible."

"Yes, and the lords are aware of it, too," Ranulf said. "Your villagers haven't been keeping the Way a secret, you see. They've been telling the neighboring villagers about it whenever they go to trade or to help. It's all over the district now—villages in five lords' demesnes."

"They've been talking about the marvelous sages who have been teaching them, too," Conn said. "A dozen villages know your names and look toward this mountain for some trace of you."

Gar stiffened. "How long before the lords send their soldiers to get rid of us?"

"Right after they punish the villagers," Ranulf said. "They've sent guards in serfs' garb to throw magical powder into the village ovens. They think one good round of vomiting and stomach cramps will make the serfs remember their places again."

Gar leaped to his feet. "We have to stop them!"

"Yes, we have to!" Alea jumped up, too. "But how? We can run down to our nearest village and tell them not to bake, but what about the other villages?"

"Conn and Ranulf can tell them," Gar said, then turned to the two ghosts. "No, wait—you said a dozen villages, and there's only two of you. Can you recruit some other friendly phantoms?"

"We've a score standing by itching for some action," Conn said with a grin. "More excitement they've ever seen this side of the grave."

"Send them to scare the serfs into keeping the grain out of the oven, would you?"

"Gladly, O Sage! Come on, Ranulf, we're heralds now!"

The two ghosts vanished. Gar turned to the younger members. "Smother the fire and come running! We're going to need to knock on every door, and quickly!" He set off downslope with Alea beside him.

Blaize stared after him, on fire with jealousy. Here he'd been studying ghost-leading for five years, and Gar came from nowhere and in five weeks could talk the specters into doing anything he wanted! Well, maybe the big man would teach what he had learned, and in any event, the people had to be warned.

The campfire burst into a ball of steam that hissed like a thousand snakes. Blaize turned to see Mira holding a bucket mouth-down over the drowned coals. "Quickly!" she told him.

"Aye." Blaize caught up the thick sheet of bark they used for a hearth-shovel and gouged up dirt to smother what had already drowned. Then he and Mira set off downhill after their teachers.

They knew they were too late as soon as they reached the village. Smoke from the oven fire lay like a pall over the common instead of spiraling up as it usually did. People were on their knees doubled over in that haze, retching miserably—men, women, children, old folk. Only Gar and Alea stood upright, but they stood in the midst of the people, the smoke had cleared around them, and two by two the serfs' heaving slackened, then ceased.

Blaize skidded to a stop. "What can we do here?"

"Aid those whose spasms have stopped! They are sorely weakened!" Mira dashed out to help one old woman who was trying to climb back to her feet.

But some sixth sense, or perhaps the touch of a ghost's warning, held Blaize to the spot, his mind seeking. He felt doom hover and, from what Gar had told him, the apprehension might not be his. He wished fervently that he could read minds as Gar and Alea could, but since he couldn't, he used what gifts he had. "Unseen ones! Ancestors of these folk! Seek, I pray you, and find the enemies who descend upon us!"

He stood stiffly, every sense alert, feeling as though he were a vibrating string on a minstrel's lute. Finally the wind came to make him thrum, a breathy voice that sighed by his ear, "They advance down the northern slope, five magicians and their guards."

"Sixty-five in all! I shall alert our own magicians!" Blaize sent all the emotion he could behind his words. "I pray you, for your descendants' sakes, slow the enemy if you can!"

"They move, they come," the ghost warned him. A sound like a breeze told Blaize it had left, hopefully to harry the magicians.

He ran to Gar and Alea, pointing toward the northern slope, "The enemy comes!"

Gar turned to see the magicians striding down the slope, blue robes fluttering, each with his dozen guards behind him. He looked down at Alea, who nodded. They turned toward their enemies and the smoke from the common streamed away toward the magicians and their soldiers. In seconds, the common was clear.

The magicians halted so suddenly that their guards bumped into them. Then they turned, plowing through their troops upslope, away from the smoke—but the wind moved faster and the cloud engulfed them, settling over magicians and guards alike. Still some blundered uphill, no doubt holding their breaths, but most sank to their knees, bent over and retching. A minute later the fugitives had to breathe, too, and fell as the cloud enfolded them.

But two downslope magicians and their guards struggled to their feet and staggered farther down out of the cloud. There they drew great lungfuls of fresh air. "Onward!" one magician croaked, pointing at Gar and Alea. A fat electrical spark burst from his fingertip and sailed toward them—but winked out halfway there. Nonetheless, he staggered toward them, and his guards pulled themselves together and followed at an unsteady gait. The other magician straightened as much as he could and came after.

It was Pilochin.

Something snapped inside Blaize. He ran toward the woozy throng, crying, "Vengeance! Vengeance for a dishonorable battle, for a kindly lord dead though a dastardly trick!"

Pilochin looked up, startled, then narrowed his eyes and panted, "You had better . . . learn from . . . his example . . . boy, and . . . flee while you can."

"Justice!" Blaize pointed straight-armed at Pilochin. "O spirits of this village, ancestors of those beset, give me justice for a good lord slain through treachery!"

Banshees howled, and the air suddenly filled with a score of ghosts, whirling like a tornado, their funnel narrowing to aim at Pilochin. The magician stumbled backward, crying out in alarm. Then the tornado struck and he shouted in pain and surprise as he fell backward sprawling on the ground. He scrambled to his feet and turned to flee in a ragged run. His guards stared at him, looked back at the host of ghosts, then threw down their weapons and followed their lord.

"Drive him mad if you can!" Blaize howled. "Chase him off the edge of a precipice!"

The ghosts might indeed manage that, he realized, for they closed in upon the magician and his guards on three sides, herding them with cries and moans and dreadful shrieks. In panic the men fled up the mountainside, tottering and gasping, weak from the retching. Some fell but kept on, crawling upslope away from the furies that followed.

Mira stared at Blaize in astonishment. He stood rigid, fists clenched, face distorted with anger.

The cloud of poisoned smoke drifted on up the mountainside, enfolding Pilochin and his men, though it was thinning rapidly. They began to retch again, but they kept staggering away from the village.

The other three magicians knelt gasping for air; so did their guards. One magician, though, managed to summon the strength to turn toward the village, raising an arm in command, then snapping it down as though hurling something—and half a dozen two-foot-long dragons sprang from the branches of the trees around the village.

Screaming, the wyverns plunged at Gar and Alea, talons extended.

11

─══ঊ৹ঊ══─

Gar and Alea looked up at the screams. So did Mira—and her blood ran cold, for a wyvern-master had come to confer with her magician-lord Roketh once, and these were the sort of little monsters he had used to terrorize his serfs into submission. No one could fight even one such creature, let alone half a dozen!

But Alea didn't know that. She glared at the wyverns, glared harder, the tendons in her neck standing out with the strain of concentration, then shook a fist in frustration.

One wyvern swerved to follow that gesture. Three others suddenly plummeted ten feet straight down, then flapped their wings frantically to regain altitude—but the other two still stooped upon their targets. Ten feet away from Gar and Alea, they suddenly shot three-foot tongues of flame from their mouths.

Attacking her friends! Imperiling the kind protectors who had saved her! Something snapped inside Mira. She dashed out in front of her two mentors, slashing the air to wave aside the two aerial flamethrowers, screaming in rage. "Away! Leave us! Go back and pounce upon him who sent you!"

The two wyverns swerved aside, then circled high, arrowing back toward their magician. He stared, dumbfounded.

So did Mira. They had obeyed her!

Then the magician recovered and pointed at his wyverns with menace. They sheered off, circling high again, and shot back toward Gar and Alea.

They had listened to her once—they might again. "Go away! Go far from here! Go home!"

Obediently, the wyverns turned as one and glided toward the east.

"Come back!" the magician shouted. "Attack!"

The wyverns turned again, beginning to look confused.

"They don't fly as well when the air sinks beneath their wings," Gar said.

Suddenly the flock plummeted straight down, screeching in surprise and distress, and this time Mira saw grass and leaves shooting outward in a circle beneath them. But there was no time to wonder—the wyverns were flapping mightily, trying to regain altitude, clawing their way back into the air.

"Tell them to roost and sleep," Gar said helpfully.

Mira didn't stop to protest that the little dragons wouldn't listen to her, only threw her hands up, crying, "Sleep! Let slumber shield you from confusion! Each seek a perch! Roost! Sleep!"

The wyverns managed to catch enough air beneath their wings to start gliding again. For a minute, they milled about in the air, uncertain what to do.

"Attack!" the magician screamed. "Fall upon them!"

"Sleep!" Mira cried.

The wyverns churned in a wobbly globe, completely confused now.

"Sleep untangles the knot of confusion!" Mira called. "Sleep sends you peace! Sleep frees you from the commands of the tyrant!"

The flock turned and shot off toward the trees.

Mira lowered her arms, staring after them. Had she really done that? What? And how? There their master stood, howling at them and waving his arms, but they paid him not the slightest heed! Had she freed the wyverns from his spell? Impossible!

Livid, the magician pointed at her. "It is you who have done this, unnatural wench! Men of mine! Set upon her!"

His guardsmen looked up in trepidation, then struggled to their feet, still green-faced and stumbling—but stumbling toward Mira.

"Well now, we can't have that," Gar said.

"Indeed not," Alea agreed. "But what can we do? Smoke was all I could handle yet, and I was surprised I could do that."

"It would seem you are telekinetic after all, but it will take a while before you can trip a dozen men like these."

"Why not?" Alea asked practically. "They're nearly falling as it is."

"A good point," Gar said. "Try twisting the back foot as it comes forward, so the toe catches on the heel of the front foot— like this." He pointed at the man on the right-hand end of the line, who promptly tripped and fell.

"Like that, is it? Well, now, let me see." Alea's face went tense with concentration again, and another man stumbled.

"Very good," Gar said. "Let me demonstrate again."

The man on the left end tripped and went sprawling.

"Oh—lead foot, you mean!" Alea glowered again at the man who had stumbled. This time, he tripped and fell.

"Very good!" Gar cried with delight. "You've learned the trick of it! Again, now!" He pointed at the left-hand end of the line once more and the next man tripped and fell.

Alea nodded and glared. The third man on the right went face-first in the grass. Then, in rapid succession, the other seven stretched their lengths on the greensward. Some of them looked up, glancing around apprehensively, but most didn't even do that. They had been fairly felled and felt no obligation to stand up and put themselves in the path of magic again.

"Up, you cowards!" their master screamed, turning purple. "Up, whoresons! Up, or face the whip!"

"I can't trip him," Alea said, her voice strained with effort. "He's not moving."

"Yes, but he's not all that steady on his feet, either," Gar pointed out. "His stomach might start twisting again."

The magician suddenly clapped his hands to his midriff, bending forward, face turning from purple to green.

"Then once he's off balance, it doesn't take much of a push to knock him down," Gar explained.

The magician tottered and fell. He clawed his way back to his feet, still bent over and holding his belly, then turned and stumbled away toward the eastern road.

One of his soldiers saw him and croaked, "We must follow and ward our lord!" He pushed himself to his feet and staggered after the magician. Faces lighting with hope, the others clambered up and followed, tottering.

Gar and Alea stood watching with satisfaction as the last of the magicians and soldiers beat a very undignified retreat. Mira and Blaize watched, too, in utter astonishment.

"Of course, they won't be willing to let it go at that," Alea told Gar.

"Indeed not," Gar agreed. "They'll be back with several more magicians and a much larger number of soldiers."

"Then what will we do?" Blaize asked, suddenly realizing the enormity of what he had already done.

"Fight them," Gar said simply, "or help them to fight themselves, which is pretty much what we did today."

Blaize's gaze drifted off as he reviewed the events of the last half-hour. "You're right! We didn't really attack them, did we? Just turned their own foul tricks back on them."

"That's how the Way defends you," Alea said, smiling. "Restore harmony, restore the beginning state of things, and the ones who clash with it fall down."

"After all," Gar said, "you seem to have a far greater number of allies than you realized."

"You mean the ghosts? Why . . . I simply thought that the ancestors of the village might want to defend their great-grandchildren," Blaize said.

Gar nodded. "You thought. That's the main thing. You seem to have acquired a much stronger knack of persuading phantoms."

"I . . . I have, haven't I?" Blaize said, nonplussed. "Does that have anything to do with the Way?"

"Maybe a little," Gar said judiciously. "You're beginning to see everything as connected, part of a single vast system—stopped seeing people and houses as being alone and separate. You looked for connections, for ghosts who had an interest in the villagers, and saw how to incite them to help defend their descendants."

Alea turned to Mira. "You didn't tell us you were a wyvern-handler."

"I didn't know," the girl said, feeling numb. "My . . . my lord Roketh . . . perhaps I watched more closely than I knew when his visitor managed his wyverns."

"Or had a talent you didn't know about."

"I don't want it!" Mira cried. "Wyverneers use their creatures to torment serfs! The people in the cities are all witches, and each has a familiar in the form of a wyvern riding on his shoulder! I won't be one of them!"

"Maybe it's like other kinds of magic," Alea suggested, "not evil in itself, but only a power, able to be used for good or for ill. They're not demons, no matter what the rumors say about the cities—they're just animals." She turned to Gar. "I still say they're pterodactyls, even though they have muzzles instead of beaks."

"And breathe fire?"

Alea shrugged. "Terra only produced fossils. How do we know pterodactyls didn't?"

"And how?" Gar mused. "I suppose their bodies manufacture methane and they exhale it to get it out of their systems."

"For all we know, pterodactyls might have," Alea said. "Monitor lizards belch a horrible-smelling gas when they fight."

Mira and Blaize stared at them, completely lost. Blaize fastened every word into his memory, though. It was magicians' talk, and someday he would understand it.

"They do have tails with broad triangular points at the ends and ridges along their backbones," Gar said. "Rudders and stabilizers, no doubt." He shrugged. "Who said evolution had to produce the same life-forms on every planet?"

"But it would produce the same ecological niches," Alea said, "and similar creatures to fill them." She turned back to Mira. "You really should develop that gift."

"Yes, you should," Blaize said, with heartfelt emotion, "for all our sakes."

Mira turned to stare at him, feeling flattered and amazed. "I—I'll try."

"So should you," Gar said to Alea. "I *thought* you had some ability for telekinesis."

"But it didn't work with their weapons!" Alea objected.

"Just a matter of practice," Gar said airily. "You were able to control the smoke because its particles have so much less mass. Start making breezes, then ripples in ponds."

"I think we've been making enough ripples as it is! Did you see the look on Pilochin's face when that tornado of ghosts hit him?"

"Yes, and I was wondering about that." Gar frowned. "If he's the man who defeated Blaize's master, he should certainly know what ghosts can and can't do."

"Oh, he knows all right," Blaize said darkly, "knows that ghosts can scare you and read your mind and make you feel emotions you've never felt, but he didn't know they could knock him down." He swallowed heavily. "Neither did I."

"Yes, you did say they couldn't do physical harm," Alea mused. "They were awfully angry, though."

"And there were a great many of them," Mira reminded.

Gar nodded. "That much emotion coming from that many ghosts—no wonder it seemed to have a physical impact."

"And if those specters could strike him down," Alea asked softly, "what else could they do?"

They looked at one another in silence for a moment, letting the question sink in. Then Gar said, "Probably not much, or they would have done it before this. But it was a very useful surprise."

"Once," Alea pointed out. "Next time, they'll be braced for it."

"Yes, but they'll also be a great deal more cautious."

"More circumspect even than these?" Gar nodded toward a handful of villagers who were coming toward them, hats in their hands.

Alea turned to them with a smile. "Come closer, friends. We are only the neighbors who have been talking with you these past weeks, nothing more."

"A great deal more," said an older woman as she stepped up. "Either that, or this Tao you speak of has much greater power than we realized."

"It has immense power," Alea said carefully, "because it is all around you and within you. Knowing how to let your enemies turn that power against themselves, though, is another matter altogether."

"Then teach it to us!" said a middle-aged man.

"That could take years," Gar cautioned.

"We can't stay among you that long," Alea added. "We have other villages to visit."

"But we can teach you how to build the foundation," Gar said, "show you ways in which you can become a stumbling block to your enemies."

"We will learn!" the woman avowed. "Only show us!"

"Then you must remember that you are all parts of one whole," Alea told her, "and treat one another as parts of yourselves."

The villagers frowned, nodding, struggling to understand.

"Come, then!" Gar turned and started back up the hillside. "Those who want to learn, come and listen!"

Half the village followed him and Alea as they climbed.

Mira and Blaize waited until the villagers had passed, then brought up the rear. They climbed beside each other in an awkward silence.

Finally Mira broke it. "I—I was amazed that you were so very angry with that tyrant Pilochin."

"He slew my master, and that not in fair combat but by an underhanded trick." Blaize's face set in hard lines. "That outraged me."

"But you seemed enraged by all of them."

"Why not? They're all just as bad as Pilochin. Any magician is who uses his powers to grind down his peasants and make them give him every luxury they can."

Mira stared at him in wonder. "You mean it!"

"Of course I mean it," Blaize said bitterly. "I am the son of serfs and would have been a serf myself if Arnogle hadn't taken me for his apprentice. He taught me more than his magic—he taught me compassion and respect for the poor. He taught me to help them make their lives as comfortable as lord and serf together could manage. He taught me to live modestly myself so that there would be more left for my people."

Mira didn't dare say it aloud, but she found herself wondering if he might be honestly dedicated to the welfare of the poor. "If you truly think that," she said, "why have you worked to master such weak creatures as ghosts, when you might have managed such mighty beings as wyverns?"

Blaize looked up in surprise. "Because I have no gift with wyverns, and I have with ghosts. It is not a matter of knowledge alone, but of talent."

"If you have talent with the one, you have talent with the other!"

"No wyvern has yet come to my call," Blaize said dubiously, "though I will admit I have only shouted at them to be gone, never to come. Still, I think this night has proved that ghosts can be as mighty as beasts."

"Only by frightening people, and soldiers grow harder and harder to frighten!"

"They grow harder and harder armor, too." Blaize was beginning to be irritated; he had done nothing to deserve this attack.

Mira, on the other hand, was surprised to discover that she no longer feared him—well, not much, anyway. "They have not yet armored their faces and would be nearly blinded if they wore iron masks to protect them from wyverns' claws!"

"There is small reason," Blaize countered, "when they can shoot down wyverns with their arrows. You cannot shoot down a ghost."

"Oh, so now you would shoot down my poor little dragonlings, would you?"

"Not I," Blaize said, totally taken aback. "But ghosts need not fear arrows."

"Then your ghosts will shoot my wyverns?"

Blaize wondered when they had become "her" wyverns. "Ghosts have nothing against the little dragons—well, I suppose there might be one or two who suffered at their claws when alive. Most phantoms are more likely to attack soldiers than wyverns."

"Maybe you should have your ghosts protect my fliers, then," Mira said with full sarcasm.

"What a splendid idea!" Blaize turned away to gaze off into the distance. "They have a common enemy, after all: magicians. How could I fashion that alliance?"

Mira stared at him, astounded. He seemed to have totally forgotten her, to become immersed in a new problem. She turned away, fuming, and hurried on uphill away from Blaize.

He came back out of the clouds to stare at her back, feeling sadness settle upon him. For a moment, he had thought she had forgiven him for being a magician, or for wanting to be one. Now, though, the anger and disgust seemed to be back. Certainly she couldn't have argued so hotly against his ghost-leading if she didn't have even more contempt for him than for other magicians—no doubt because she knew him personally.

He sighed and plowed on up the hill, trying to find refuge in the new problem of a wyvern-ghost alliance, but failing. Mira's face kept coming into his mind no matter how he tried to banish it—her lip twisted with scorn, her eyes flashing anger. She was the loveliest creature he had ever met, but he would have to give up all hope of winning her. She clearly didn't even like him, let alone love him.

It was definitely better to pledge his life to his art. With an immense effort, he began to contemplate the natures of ghosts and wyverns. For one thing, they had both been here on this world before his ancestors had come from the stars—or at least the wild ghosts had, though not their Terran forms. Could that be bond enough?

He felt the fascination of the problem closing over him like a shield and strode uphill, following his teachers.

The subject came up again that evening, when the villagers had gone home to prepare their evening meal. Alea said, "You know, we might have lost that battle if Mira hadn't been able to turn the wyverns away."

"We might indeed." Gar didn't seem completely confident in his own ability to have dealt with the reptiles. He turned to Mira. "You really must develop that talent."

"Become a magician?" Mira said, horrified.

"For your own defense, and to protect these villagers? Yes, I think you should," Alea said.

"But I don't want to become a tyrant!"

"Then don't," Gar said simply. "Having power doesn't mean you absolutely must abuse it, after all."

"I suppose there is truth in that." Mira tried to ignore the gleam in Blaize's eyes. "But how could I go about learning?"

"I would say trial and error," Gar said, "but the errors could prove very painful. The wyverns' teeth looked sharp and their claws rather strong."

"They say a flock of them can tear apart an armed soldier," Mira said, and shuddered.

Blaize nodded gravely. "I saw it happen once, before Arnogle's ghosts put the creatures to flight."

Mira turned to him in surprise. "Ghosts can banish wyverns?"

Blaize spread his hands. "It must be as you said—both are

native to this world, and like listens to like, even if the ghosts' guise is human."

"Ghosts . . ." Alea said thoughtfully. "What if we could bring the ghost of a wyvern-handler here?" She turned to Mira. "Would you be willing to learn from such a one?"

Mira shrank back, then mustered her courage, tilted her chin up, and said, "I would, if you could find such a ghost who had a good heart."

"It's worth trying," Gar said slowly. "Blaize, see if any of our friendly neighborhood ghosts are hanging around, would you?"

Blaize's eyes lost focus as his mind called, *Conn—Ranulf—if you are near, please appear.*

"Should we let them know we were listening?" Conn's voice asked out of the dusk.

"No. Let them think we only come if they ask." Ranulf's form began to coalesce against the darkness of the cliff face.

"Let me guess." Conn appeared near the fire. "You wondered if we knew any wyvern-handlers who happened to be conveniently dead."

"I wouldn't think death could be convenient," Gar said, "but other than that, yes. You're very skilled eavesdroppers."

"It comes naturally, when you can be invisible," Conn said airily. He turned to his friend. "What do you say, Ranulf—Goedelic? That little old outlaw who haunts the cliff face in the Brogenstern Mountains?"

"He's crusty but kind." Ranulf nodded thoughtfully. "Of course, no one ever called him a magician. You don't, generally, when it's an outlaw who has discovered he can work magic."

"Yes, but there was Lord Starchum," Conn reminded. "He took over the whole forest, then used the outlaw army to overthrow Lord Imbroglio."

"Well, yes," Ranulf conceded, "but he was a fire-caster. Outlaws in the greenwood pay attention to that kind of thing. Still, are you sure Goedelic is the best teacher for the lass? That middle-aged woman's ghost by the River Ripar—wouldn't she be a better teacher in this case?"

"Well, she's honest and no tyrant," Conn said thoughtfully, "but she's not very pleasant. Abrupt, too. I don't think she'd be very patient with a beginner's first fumbling steps. No, I'll go find Goedelic." He started to fade.

"No, please!" Gar held up a hand. "Just connect with another ghost who can connect with a third ghost to whom he can pass the message. Then the third can add a fourth and so on, until Goedelic hears and answers."

"Ah! Your ghost-to-ghost network!" Conn said brightly. "Yes, why not put it to the test?" He gazed off into space for a moment, then smiled. "Roigel answered. The message is on its way."

Suddenly the fire belched a massive cloud of smoke, which thickened as it drifted aside and took on the contours of a human form and face. "Why would you be wanting to contact Goedelic?" a booming voice asked.

12

Gar blinked. "Am I talking to an Irish ghost?"

"I wouldn't be knowing. Are you?" The cloud rotated toward him, rapidly solidifying into the face and form of a middle-aged warrior with a huge tear over the chest of his tunic. His nose was a bulb, his hair a fringe around a bald head, his chin a knob. His chubby face seemed made for smiling. At the moment, though, it was set in stern lines.

"I would say I am," Gar said, "by your accent."

"Accent? What accent would that be? Everybody talks like this in my parish!" the ghost said. "Faith, it's yourself that has an accent!"

"Him, and all the rest of the world," Conn grunted, and Ranulf laughed.

The Irish ghost turned toward them, raising a knobbed stick. "Be showing some respect, or you'll have a taste of my shillelagh!"

"It looks like licorice," Ranulf said.

"No, chocolate." Conn grinned. "Come on, old fellow! You know we can't hurt one another after we're dead. Who are you and why did you answer a call for Goedelic? For that matter, *what* are you—outlaw or soldier?"

"It's all of us were warriors in my day," the Irishman answered. "There was none of this business of outlaws or soldiers, for we were all free! If any magician tried to set himself up as a lord, we taught him the right of it, and quickly, too!"

Conn and Ranulf lost their smiles. "How old an ancestor *are* you?"

"Four centuries it is that I've been dead," the Irishman said, "or what passes for death here. As to my name, it's Corley, and Goedelic's my great-great-grandson! Degenerate times, when the people let magicians scare them into obeying! But Goedelic fought against them to the last, he with his wyverns, and I'll not have you tormenting his rest!"

"I don't think the ghost-to-ghost hookup worked," Alea said.

Gar shrugged. "There's always interference."

Corley turned toward him with a menacing glare. "What were you calling me?"

"We didn't—we called for Goedelic," Gar answered.

"But now that we have a ghost from such an early time," Alea said, "maybe you can explain something that's been troubling me."

"Now, why should I be doing that?"

"Only out of kindness to a damsel."

Corley fixed her with a glittering eye. His mouth began to curve in an appreciative smile. "Well, could be I would at that, for one so comely as yourself."

"Why, thank you," Alea said, blushing.

Gar glanced from her to Corley, frowning.

Surely he couldn't be jealous of a ghost! But the thought gave Alea a bit of a glow as she said, "This world of Oldeira seems to have had a very promising beginning—"

"Aye, but the promise was broken in my grandfather's time."

"I was wondering how that happened," Alea said. "All your people seemed to be born with the same chances at the start of their lives, or as close to that as any society can manage. Even when they were grown up they treated each other as equals and fellows. Everyone seemed to have been tolerant of everyone else's views and respected each other's religions."

"What would religion be?" asked the Irishman.

Alea stared, then recovered. "The . . . the worship of a supreme being, and living in accord with the principles that Being revealed."

"Oh." Corley rolled his eyes up, rubbing his chin. "No, I don't think you could say we had religions as such. Philosophies, now, that would be another matter, an understanding of how everything fitted together into a grand whole that might and might not be a Being. Mind you, there were some that worshipped their ancestors—but you can understand that, when those ancestors were apt to come calling any night."

"Uh, yes, I suppose so," Alea said, feeling rather numb. "But how could such a free and earnest society have broken down into this patchwork of tyrannies enforced by the 'magic' of trickery and a few psi powers?"

"Ah, how does the old saying go?" Corley mused. " 'There's a sucker born every minute.' "

" 'And two to take him,' " Conn and Ranulf chorused.

"You wouldn't be those two, would you?"

The ghostly duo only grinned in response.

"Don't overreach yourselves, lads," Corley warned. "That saying is far older than any of us, and you'd have to be rapscallions indeed to be deserving of it." He turned back to Alea. "I only know what my old grandad told me—that the people lost the habit of skepticism. When you stop testing claims by reason and evidence, you're apt to believe anything that sounds impressive, and when it's something you see, well! You're going to believe it, bad or good."

"But you had schools, educated people . . ." Alea's voice trailed off.

Corley wagged a finger at her. "Don't confuse education with sound judgment, colleen. Maybe the two should go together, but they don't when the teacher stops showing proof and the students stop thinking ideas through."

"Surely that's too simple an explanation," Gar objected. "You were cut off from the mother planet, thrown back on your own resources. Didn't that have anything to do with it?"

"Ah, well, of course it did!" Corley said. "Desperate people will seize hold of anything that promises them a full belly and a safe house—and what are they to do when the man to whom they give power doesn't keep those promises? But I'm only guessing, you see—I wasn't there."

"I . . . don't suppose there's any chance that . . . you could arrange it so that we could talk to ghosts who lived through it, is there?" Alea asked. She fluttered her eyelashes for good measure.

Corley gave her a knowing grin. "For so pretty a colleen as yourself? Sure and I will! But be wary—what you get may not be what you think you've wished for!" He disappeared suddenly and completely.

Alea stared. "Where has he gone?"

"To find a friend who was alive when things fell apart, I expect," Conn said.

Ranulf said to Gar, "You may have hooked up your ghosts more thoroughly than you knew."

Corley burst upon the scene like an exploding firecracker, arm in arm with the ghost of an old woman wearing a long skirt and a voluminous shawl over a blouse. Her hair was wrapped in a kerchief, her lean and lined old face was wrinkled and, even in the colorless glow of her spectral form, seemed leathery. "Is this the lass, then?" she demanded in a voice like the cry of a jay.

"I—I am the young woman who asked to speak with one of the oldest ghosts, yes," Alea said, taken aback by the old woman's energy. "My name is Alea."

"Odd name." The crone sniffed. "Still, mine is Lodicia, so who am I to talk? Corley tells me you wondered how our wonderful world fell apart."

"I'm curious, yes. So many things about the way you lived seem so very right. Did you live through the collapse?"

"No, but I saw it as a ghost, and disgusting it was, I can tell you!" the old woman said. "Mind you, we had gurus and chelas— teachers and students, to you—even when we came here, but there were philosophers, too, and they had great and wonderful debates, teaching us all to think through the issues for ourselves!"

"When you came here?" Alea's eyes widened. "Are you one of the original colonists?"

"That I was, though I was in the third ship. By the time we came, the streets were laid out and some of the houses already built. The farms were producing, of course—the first ship saw to that."

"How many ships were there?" Gar asked.

"Twenty there were—one a year, each with five thousand immigrants aboard. Everyone who wanted to go to a world where philosophy was the only king, where cooperation was prized above competition, where people ruled themselves and worked out their differences by talking in councils—well, you'd be surprised how many there were who were eager to leave old Terra to come here."

Alea stared off into space with a haunted gaze and Gar knew

she was remembering the oppression and constant warfare of her home world. "I can believe it," she said.

Lodicia's eyebrows rose in surprise. "Then you won't believe how quick our grandchildren were to turn away from it."

"Every generation tries to establish its identity by rejecting some of the ideas of its elders," Gar said with a haunted look of his own.

"Yes, well, it was our children who were the cause of it, really—I shouldn't blame the grandchildren for listening to them," Lodicia allowed. "Some of them became gurus in their own turn, of course, we expected that, wanted that—but we didn't look for a dozen of them to get hungry for power and try to seize it by gathering young lonely ones about them to pay them virtual worship."

"They rejected reason, then," Gar said with a frown.

"Yes, and rejected with it the idea that all people are only that, people—that there aren't any prophets or reborn saints," Lodicia said bitterly. "One of my own grandchildren joined such a cult. Oh, his guru played right smartly on his followers, awing them with fireballs that were no more than flash powder and mind reading that was no more than the old vaudeville mentalists' tricks! But the worst came when one of them died and sent his ghost to overawe his worshippers. Then his son really had them by the hindbrain, with an actual ghost to conjure!"

Light exploded near her with a boom that shook the leaves about them. Blaize leaped up in a fighter's crouch. Mira was on her feet, too, ready to run but waiting to see if she should.

Gar and Alea sat still, though, staring at the apparition that appeared next to Lodicia: an old man in a robe and pointed hat embroidered with zodiacal symbols. His beard fell down over his chest, his hair around his shoulders. "Why don't you tell them the rest of it, old woman? About the tractors that wouldn't work because Terra wouldn't send us any more parts, the ethanol distilleries that had to shut down, the famine that stalked the land as we reinvented plowing with horses and oxen!"

"Yes, all of that happened, Aesc," Lodicia said, her lip curling, "but that didn't give you the right to set yourself up as a petty tyrant."

"Right? It was my duty!" Aesc exclaimed. "Everything was falling apart when Terra cut us off! No one knew how to repair the machines, or what to do when the villages couldn't talk with the towns anymore, to call for help or to plan! Everyone swarmed out of the cities, leaving only the idiots and the deformed to hunt for nuts and squirrels to eat! People were starving, whole villages were turning bandit and stealing other villages' food! Someone had to gather people together and show them how to farm like primitives! Someone had to overawe the bandits and chase them away! We were one step away from turning into a feudal society with all its oppression!"

"So you beat them to it and made lords of the magicians, instead of the warriors," Lodicia said with scathing sarcasm.

"Wasn't it the better way?" Aesc demanded. "Now, instead of lords leading armies to kill each other by the hundreds, we had magicians with scarcely a score of soldiers battling it out by illusions and tricks!"

"And how were you to know that some of you had turned into telepaths and were making your tricks deadly?" Lodicia sneered.

"Who could have guessed that could happen in only three generations?" Aesc countered. "Who could have known that the strange gossamer clouds blowing through the air could turn into ghosts when dying minds seized them? Who could have known that those ghosts would select and pair up people who had ESP talents? It's not as though we set out to become real, genuine mind readers!"

"Oh, I believe that," Lodicia said. "Tricks are so much easier to control."

"All right, the new powers became unpredictable!" Aesc admitted, thin-lipped. "Is it any surprise that even we who wielded them began to believe in the supernatural and came to call ourselves shamans instead of magicians? After all, we were healing with one hand while fighting off bandits with the other! Who could have guessed that we were really using psionic talents as much herbs and weapons? But we kept the warlords from rising!"

"You *became* warlords!" Lodicia retorted, eyes burning. "You turned into the very monsters you claimed to be fighting! What did it matter that you were using your so-called magic instead of armies? You were still petty tyrants, feudal lords!"

"Fewer people died in battle, only a handful—that's what difference it made!"

"And the only difference! You fought each other to stalemates and kept any real government from rising! You overawed the councils so that they withered away! There was no power left to protect the poor and send food from those who had plenty to those who had none! You made each magician into a petty king over his own few square miles with the power of life and death over his hundreds of people—and he wouldn't let them leave his estate, because what's a lord without somebody to browbeat? The people became serfs and the shamans became lords just as surely as though you had called yourselves dukes and earls! You were no better than any other kind of warlord— you oppressed your people just as harshly! The only thing you really changed was the kind of power you used to bully them— charlatans' magic instead of fists and clubs!"

"Scoff if you like," Aesc said, eyes blazing, "but we never did let a warlord rise and conquer his way into a kingship. Individual domains remained free!"

"Aye, the magician lords remained free, but no one else! Now the serfs dress in rags and are driven to grub in the fields so their lords can dress in velvet and loll about in their great padded chairs taking their ease! Guards still march to war at the commands of their lords! Serfs who displease you and escape your death sentences take to the forest and become bandits, harrying all the villages! You have fashioned a living nightmare from the ruins of your grandparents' dream!"

Before Aesc could retort, Gar said quickly, " 'Needs must as the devil drives,' as the old saying goes. Maybe the shamans made a worse choice than they could have, but they did keep the people alive, kept some vestige of civilization."

"Vestige indeed!" Lodicia said indignantly. "Can you really call it civilization when there is no trade, no arts, no crafts more skilled than rough carpentry?"

"Civilization is the way of life of people who live in cities," Alea put in.

"Yes, and there are no cities here, only mansions and villages!"

"But there is a basis for civilization to grow again," Gar said in as soothing a tone as he could manage. "A crystal city may still grow from the ruins."

"How, as long as the magicians block any power but their own?" Lodicia asked bitterly.

"By reviving the power of your dream," Alea answered. "If we can teach the villages to cooperate again, they will outdo the power of the lords' conflicts."

Aesc eyed her narrowly but said nothing, only listened.

"How are you to do that?" Lodicia demanded.

"By learning how to command wyverns, for a beginning," Alea answered. "We have a young woman here who has discovered she has a talent for it—discovered it rather abruptly and rudely, at that. Can you find us the ghost of a wyvern-handler to teach her?"

"What! Raise up one more magician?" Lodicia cried.

"I will never be a magician!" Mira said hotly.

Lodicia chopped the denial aside with a wave of her hand. "If you learn to work magic, you are a magician."

"But I will never oppress the poor! I will use my gift to make their lives better, sweeter!"

"So said many who are now lords," Lodicia said sourly, "and look what power has done to them."

"Surely taming beasts is not truly magic," Aesc objected, "no matter how supernatural their appearance. If the lass uses wyverns to protect the poor, can you really object?"

Lodicia gave him a simmering glare while she looked for the flaw in his argument. At last she said, "It takes a talent, you can't deny that. What's the difference between talent and magic?"

"When I look at the paintings of the masters and listen to the symphonies of the great composers, I have to agree with you," Gar said. "Still, I don't think their magic is quite the same thing as throwing fireballs or raising hosts of ghosts."

Lodicia glowered at him but didn't answer.

"She is a serf," Alea reminded the crone's ghost, "and means to send wyverns to defend serfs' villages."

"Perhaps," Lodicia allowed, then turned on Mira with eyes that flamed. "Though mind you, girl, if you betray your fellows with this power, I shall haunt you for the rest of your days!"

"Do so." Mira bore up bravely under her glare. "If I should so forget the hurts my people have borne, I could deserve no less."

Still Lodicia held her stare, but the fire in her eyes faded until they only glowed. Then she gave a single nod. "Well enough, then. I shall summon Hano." She scowled more deeply than ever.

The companions waited, holding their breaths.

13

A patch of fog gathered next to Lodicia, thickened, then formed itself into the ghost of a man in his forties wearing doublet and hose beneath his cloak and a hat with a jaunty feather. He held his forearm up with the ghost of a wyvern perched on it, hissing as it coiled and uncoiled its tail. "Where is she who would command my dragons?" Hano cried gaily.

"I—I am she." Mira swallowed and took a step forward, almost succeeding in hiding her trembling.

"Are you, then? Don't be afeard, lass—if you've the gift, they'll not hurt you."

It wasn't the wyverns hurting her that worried Mira, but she didn't tell the ghost that.

"Though, mind you," Hano said, "you'll need a stout gauntlet, such as this." He held out his forearm for her to see. He wore a leather glove with a thick, stiff cuff that extended almost up to his elbow. "You'll need leather for your shoulders, too, if you want them to perch." He gestured to the shoulders of his doublet, which were indeed thickened.

Mira shrank away at the warning.

"Not that you need to have them sit there," Hano said quickly. "You can bid one perch anywhere near you—that tree limb, for example." He pointed at the nearest branch. "Go on, go over there. Stand near, but not too near."

With several glances at him, Mira went, though her footsteps dragged.

"There's a brave lass!" Hano cried. "Now call for a wyvern."

"How—how do I do that?"

"With your mind, lass, your thoughts alone, though you can speak them aloud if that helps. Go on, now, sing its praises. Tell it what a beautiful beast it is, how its scales shine and its eyes glow—you know, flattery. Works with every animal."

"Including man," Alea muttered.

"In both sexes," Gar qualified.

"But . . . but I can't even see one!" Mira protested.

"Doesn't matter," Hano told her. "Think of a wyvern, any wyvern. Doesn't even have to be a real one. Think of Gorak, here."

The ghostly wyvern gave a raucous cry.

"All—all right." Mira screwed her eyes up tight, clenched her fists, and went rigid. Minutes passed. Blaize started toward her, his face a mask of concern, but Gar held out a hand to stop him.

"How does she?" Lodicia asked in an anxious undertone.

"Well, she's thinking it right," Hano answered softly. "Now we'll see if she has the talent, as you told me . . . There!"

He pointed at a speck in the sky. It swelled as it plunged, growing wings and a long supple neck. As it took on the shape of a dragon, several other specks appeared.

"Talent, truly!" Hano declared. "She's called not just one, but half a dozen!"

In no time at all, it seemed, Mira had six wyverns perched

side by side on the branch and Blaize was frantically cutting scraps from the bones of last night's dinner for her to toss to her new friends.

"They don't mind it smoked or dried," Hano told her, "so it's best to keep a pouch of tidbits by you at all times. Think now of an errand you'd like it to run and the juicy bit of meat it will have if it does. No, don't close your eyes—once they're here, you need to keep watch on them."

"But . . . but how can I picture something in my mind if my eyes are open?"

"By practice, lass. Come now, I didn't say it would be easy. Watch the wyverns but think of one of them flying away and coming back, nothing more."

Mira's face tensed with strain, but she stared at the wyvern on the left end until it took off in an explosion of wings, caught a thermal and rose in lazy loops, then arrowed off to the west, turned in a long curve, and came sailing back. It landed on the branch again, jaws gaping for its reward. Mira threw it a gobbet of meat.

"Well done!" Hano cried. "The next one, now."

He coaxed, cajoled, and taught. Mira listened with single-minded intensity, and in the process lost her fear of ghosts.

The villagers came to learn in droves after that. Seeing their new sages fight off five magicians left them with a great desire to learn. They listened intently and even began trying to apply Taoist principles in everyday life. As Gar and Alea taught them, that included striving for harmony within themselves and without—in practical terms, such things as planning instead of worrying and turning quarrels into discussions. Of far more interest to the serfs was the instruction in martial arts, showing them how they could respond to attack by using an opponent's strength and momentum to help him defeat himself. They understood quite well how that could restore harmony between bully and victim.

The exercises also helped them to balance the conflicting tensions of their bodies into inner harmony, which they felt as peace—though they didn't notice that until their teachers pointed it out to them.

They weren't the only ones who gained a new viewpoint toward their studies. After their conference with the ghosts, neither Gar nor Alea could begin to meditate without a peripheral awareness of half a dozen specters hanging on their every thought—but in a trance even that ceased to matter much.

Blaize and Mira studied and practiced as assiduously as any of the villagers—more, considering that, after the countryfolk had left, the two of them worked at developing their different talents. Blaize was indignant at first, still offended that Gar and Alea should so easily succeed where he had made such slow progress.

"It's not fair!" he told Mira. "I labored long and hard, I practiced hours every day for five years trying to attract and control ghosts and they've surpassed me in a matter of days!"

"But you didn't know the Way," Mira reminded him, "and they did."

Blaize frowned in thought, then nodded reluctantly. "Yes, that makes sense. The ghosts must be part of the Tao, too, mustn't they? Whether they know it or not. Yes, of course somebody who knew the Way would be able to learn quickly how to deal with phantoms."

"It will take us longer, of course," Mira told him. "We're both trying to learn the Way at the same time as we're trying to apply it."

"Yes. Of course we'll go more slowly." Blaize gave her a look that was almost as surprised as it was pleased. Inside, he rejoiced, amazed—Mira no longer seemed to be treating him as a villain! She even seemed friendly! He would have liked more, but he was happy with what progress he seemed to have made.

He and Mira both buckled down to some serious learning. Mira suffered a nightly training session with Hano and her friendship with wyverns, all wyverns, grew by leaps and bounds; soon there was almost nothing the little dragons wouldn't do for her.

Gar waited for the surrounding villages to come to learn the Way. When no one came, he did a telepathic survey to see if perhaps his village was the planet's best-kept secret—but no, peasant had talked to peasant who had talked to peasant, cousin to uncle to second cousin once-removed, and the surrounding villages had indeed learned what was happening here. In fact, the news seemed to be spreading far and wide, like ripples in a pond, but no one else came to learn. Gar began to realize that they were all taking the prudent course of waiting to see what happened to the villagers who had dared to learn to fight back— though of course, the serfs themselves hadn't fought their lords, only their teachers had. It remained to be seen if the magicians would punish the peasants simply for learning.

Gar realized the sense of it. "That's what I would do in their places," he confided to Alea.

"Of course," she said. "They're alive, after all. Why risk magicians coming to throw boulders and fireballs unless you know you're going to be able to fight them off?"

"I don't think the magicians will attack the village just for becoming Taoists," Gar mused, "but they might attack us."

"Yes, they might," Alea agreed. "Do we have the right to stay and endanger the village?"

"They are making excellent progress toward understanding the world without superstition—or at least as much as they can, on a planet like this." A proud smiled flickered over his face, then flickered again. "They've learned the courage of their convictions, too. They might even be willing to do what they believe to be right no matter how their lord threatened."

"Dangerous, that," Alea pointed out. "It's only a step or two from striking back at the magicians for trying to do what's wrong."

"Well, yes, but that's been my goal, hasn't it?" Gar said candidly. "Nonetheless, I don't think they can win yet, not by themselves. We'll have to convert a few more villages."

"Time to hit the road," Alea agreed.

The next morning, they came down to the village to tell their pupils good-bye.

The villagers panicked.

"But how will we live without you?" an older man cried. "The magicians will fall on us again and flay us alive for having fought them!"

"You didn't fight them," Gar pointed out. "We did."

"They're not apt to attack you by yourselves," Alea said, "especially since your lives are even more peaceful now that you've learned what we had to teach."

"Peaceful!"

"Why, yes," Gar said mildly. "I haven't heard husbands and wives screaming at each other very often in the last few weeks, and no fistfights between drunks."

"In fact, no drunks," Alea added.

The villagers looked at one another, startled.

"Well," one young man said, "we may not be having fistfights, but when Athelstan and I grew angry with each other we made it a martial arts match, as you've shown us."

"And worked off your anger with neither being hurt much." Gar nodded. "You restored harmony inside you both, and harmony between you. No magician is going to object to his serfs living in peace."

"As long as we don't practice our new skills on him, eh?" the older man said with a grin.

"Exactly. What lord ever minded his peasants indulging in a bout of wrestling now and then?"

"But the teacher's another matter," Alea said. "The magicians don't know where our doctrines might end. If we leave now, they'll be content to see you're peaceful—but if we stay, they'll come back to wipe us out."

"Or try to," Gar said, poker-faced.

All things considered, the villagers decided they were right to leave.

"*You* could stay," one old woman said to the two apprentices half-hopefully.

Mira looked at Blaize, startled, and they saw the temptation in each other's eyes.

"There's something to be said for having a home," Blaize admitted.

"Yes, but not if the lord's going to command you to do things you hate." Mira's resolve stiffened. "Besides, I haven't learned everything Alea and Gar have to teach me yet."

"Neither have I." Blaize turned to the old woman. "Thank you for the invitation, but I think I'll follow my teachers."

"I, too," Mira said, "but thank you."

"Go well, then," the old woman sighed, then admitted, "I would, if I were your age and unmarried with no children."

Off they went, to follow Gar and Alea.

The search for more pupils was depressing, though. They did just as they had, setting up camp on a hillside above a hamlet, then sitting in meditation long hours, waiting for the villagers to come spying out of curiosity—but the serfs stayed home, and after two weeks of waiting, Gar investigated mentally.

"They're not curious," he reported to Alea. "They know who we are."

"So the grapevine's been that busy, has it?" Alea asked sourly. "And they'd rather be cautious than learn?"

"All they can see is that we bring magicians on the attack," Gar said, "and that we didn't even stay around to guard the one village that did listen to us."

"Perhaps we've tried the wrong village," Alea suggested.

So they struck camp and hiked fifty miles, hoping a different demesne would have villagers with a different attitude. After two weeks with no sign of interest, though, Gar read minds again and reported, "They're afraid to take the chance of finding something better, for fear of losing what they already have."

"That isn't much," Alea said, wrinkling her nose.

"No, but they don't have magicians fighting in their pastures very often, and they don't have to worry about bandits—their lord gets angry if anyone else tries to fleece his peasants."

"That's *his* privilege," Alea said tartly.

"Of course," Gar echoed. "He thinks that's what serfs are for. But he does give them some security: they know what to expect next month, even if it's only forced labor on his lands and taxes at harvest time."

"So the villagers prefer the security of an overlord even it if means oppression and losing their young people to the magician's service—the girls to wait on him and the boys to be his guards." Alea shook her head in disgust. "I hope you're wrong."

"So do I," Gar sighed. "After all, in their own minds, they're only being prudent. I'm very much afraid, though, that they lack the courage to be free and the willingness to accept the responsibility that goes along with that freedom."

Alea thought she had never seen him look so dejected. She tried to buck him up. "It's not inborn, though. Blaize and Mira are proof of that."

"Yes, they are, aren't they?" Gar looked up at the two youngsters with a smile. "They had the courage to fight, in their own ways, and they are making progress." His smile turned sardonic. "More than I am, at the moment."

"Yes." Alea turned to beam at the younger members of the team, sitting by the fire in earnest discussion—maybe a little too earnest. "Hano's ghost tells me that Mira's a very rare kind of wyverneer. Most of them train their reptiles by rewards of meat and punishment of headaches, but that's not her style."

"Really," Gar said, interested. "How does she control them?"

"Well, she doesn't really—she just makes friends with them. They choose to fly along because they enjoy her company."

"Then they'll do anything to protect a friend?" Gar grinned. "So all she has to do is persuade them that attacking her enemies is protecting her."

"Or even bringing her a rabbit for dinner," Alea said.

Gar frowned. "I don't remember her using them to hunt."

"She says she hasn't, but they've offered time and again—something like a cat bringing you a dead mouse as a gift."

Gar smiled, amused. "Well, if we find a rabbit in the pot some night, we'll know they stopped offering and started doing. I wonder why more wyverneers don't use her approach."

"She explained it to me. She makes friends with the wild wyverns, and they're very different from the flocks born in captivity on her home estate. She says the tame wyverns are all bloodthirsty little creatures, bred and trained to be saurian sadists—attacking anything their masters tell them to, obeying anybody who's meaner than they are."

"Not the world's best news." Gar frowned.

Blaize raised his voice a notch. "Your wild wyverns may know love and loyalty, but could they stand against the blood-crazed coursers a magician raises?"

"Oh, be sure they can," Mira told him. "After all, what kinds of enemies do the tame wyverns fight? Only peasants who are frightened of them before they see them, just by what they've heard of the beasts. But your wild wyvern has to bring home dinner every day, which means he has to hunt and kill it—and fight off beasts who want to make dinner of *her!*"

"Not 'my' wild wyvern," Blaize objected. "I'll cleave to my ghosts, thank you. At least they can think about what to do or not do."

"I'll have you know my wyverns think quite well! And they're loyal—once they decide you're a friend, they're true for life!"

"How would you know? You've only had them for a few weeks," Blaize objected.

"At least they're real friends, not allies out of convenience!"

"I wouldn't call having a mutual enemy convenience—"

"Wouldn't you?" Mira challenged. "As soon as that mutual enemy's overcome, your ghosts will drift away and ignore you— if they don't find a reason to turn on you first!"

Blaize smiled. "I'll have to learn to persuade them not to, won't I?"

"My friends," Mira pointed out, "don't need persuading— not once you've befriended them, at least!"

"Hold!" Blaize raised a hand, looking off into space. "*My* friends are sounding the alarm!"

Sure enough, Conn and Ranulf appeared in the shade of an oak, dim and watery in daylight, but their faces were hard and angry. "Up and away!" Conn cried. "Your enemies are on the march!"

"How far away?" Gar came to his feet.

"Perhaps half an hour, at their rate of march. Off with you!"

Blaize and Mira leaped up in alarm.

Gar stood, scowling.

"The better part of valor," Alea reminded him.

"It's the same five magicians." Gar read distant minds, his

gaze remote under lowering brows. "But they're bringing fifty guards each this time. They're planning to let brute strength and strong brutes do the worst of the job for them."

"The worst?" Alea asked in alarm. "I thought they fought with magic!"

"Not when they're outspelled." Gar's eyes sparkled with anger. "This time they're going to sit back and wait while their little army of two hundred fifty charges in to catch us and tie us up."

"Two hundred fifty?" Conn said with a vulpine smile. "Then half of them are fresh from the plow with scarcely enough training to hold a spear! One sight of a ghost, one moan, one clank of a chain, and home they'll run!"

"He's right." Blaize squared his shoulders even though his eyes were wide with fear. "And if one ghost should scare them, a dozen will rout them utterly. I'll call up a few I've come to know—"

"And I shall summon a dozen of the friends I've made these last few weeks!" Mira cried. "Let's see how their courage holds in the face of claws—and claws in the face!" She trembled, but she stood firm.

Alea smiled at both of them, then turned back to Gar. "Do you still doubt the worth of these serfs?"

"Not these two, at least," Gar said with an answering smile, "but I don't think we can fight off this many without some getting hurt, even a man or two dead."

"Let them die!" cried Ranulf. "They knew the risk when they became soldiers!"

"Yes, but only a few of them actually chose their trade," Gar answered, "and we're preaching peace and harmony, not slaughter. We'll fight if we have to—but so far we don't have to."

Alea nodded. "Time for discretion."

"What does that mean?" Blaize asked, puzzled.

"In practical terms, it means we strike camp and see if we can march faster than the magicians' little army," Gar told him.

"You don't mean we're running away!"

"I mean exactly that," Gar said. "If they don't give up the chase, we'll choose high ground and a narrow trail to make our stand and fight them off. If we fight them here, though, the battle might spill over onto the villagers, and they may not deserve to be free, but they don't deserve to die, either."

"No, that's true," Blaize said, frowning. He turned away to start stuffing his pack.

"No amusement here," Conn said in scorn. "Let us know if you decide to stand up for yourself, laddie!"

He and Ranulf disappeared.

Mira looked up at the half-dozen wyverns circling above. "There're friends for you! I didn't even call—they came because they felt my alarm." She raised her voice. "Not yet, little ones! Go and hide, but stay near. If the soldiers attack, I'll call on you quickly."

The wyverns wheeled and glided away toward a stand of trees, squawking in disappointment.

"Not as good as ghosts, perhaps, but they certainly could prove useful," Blaize said, his eyes on the little dragons.

"Not as good! What's better about your ghosts, I'd like to know?"

"They can't be knocked out of the air by crossbow bolts, for one thing," Blaize said. "Here, I'll pack your tent. You drown the fire."

Off they went as quickly as they could into the forest and along the stream, but the woods-ghosts told Blaize that the soldiers were still coming. Slow they might be and wary of the shadows and overhanging limbs, but their masters wouldn't let them stop, driving them ahead with fire and shaking the earth behind them.

"Might bandits find us?" Mira asked, looking about them wide-eyed.

Gar gazed off into the shadows. "They already have—and they're thinking about attacking, but they realize they'd have to fight the soldiers for us. They're pulling back to watch and wait." Then he straightened, smiling. "One of them has a boat moored nearby! We'll borrow it."

They found a rowboat moored beneath an overhanging bank. In they went and took turns with the oars. The current quickened and bore them out of the forest much faster than the soldiers could march, but as they came out of the trees, they found themselves in a gully.

"Over to the side," Gar directed. "I don't like traveling where somebody can throw rocks down at me."

His friends allowed as how he had a point and moored the boat to a root. Up the bank they climbed, then across a meadow to the shadow of some hills. They climbed as the sun sank behind them, and when they reached the top, they looked down the far side and saw, in the gloom of the hills' shadow, a grim outcrop of angular shapes where two rivers met. Clusters of lights glowed in its darkness.

"A city!" Alea exclaimed, staring.

"Yes, one of the graveyards of our ancestors," Blaize said, shivering. "I wouldn't like to try to sort out the hundreds of ghosts I'd find in those towers!"

"*Somebody* lives there," Gar pointed out. "Somebody alive, I mean."

Alea looked back sharply. "Do you hear that?"

The others fell silent, listening, and heard the clank of steel behind them. They turned to look anxiously and saw Conn in the shadows below them, waving and calling, "They found your boat and are climbing after—much more quickly now that they're out of the forest!"

"Try to slow them down, will you?" Blaize asked.

"We'll try." Conn shrugged. "But their masters have ghosts of their own, and any fear we inspire will be balanced by those behind them."

Ranulf appeared beside him, calling, "Go quickly! Go to ground! Hide while you may!"

"Hide?" Blaize asked in a quandary. "Where?"

"There's a city below you to the east! They'll never come after you there."

"Neither will we!" Mira shuddered. "I've no wish to be plagued by the ghosts of our ancestors—or hunted by the maniacs who are too mad to fear them!"

"You've small choice!" Conn said impatiently. "Besides, what's to fear from a few ghosts?"

"But these are the ghosts of centuries of madmen!" Blaize protested.

"Aye, and some might have rage so intense as to cause a mortal pain," Ranulf conceded. "Still and all, lad, it's phantom pain and means nothing. Spectral swords don't really pierce you, limbs aren't truly broken. Ignore and plow ahead, and they'll leave off."

"I don't think I like the sound of this." Alea turned to Blaize. "Nonetheless, lad, I think we can summon anger to equal their own. If they can cause us pain, we can return it."

Blaize looked none too sure—in fact, he looked as fearful as a rabbit surrounded by foxes—but he swallowed, straightened his shoulders, and said bravely, "Surely we can. Let us march."

"We have some protection, at least." Mira looked up and a dozen wyverns came flocking, cawing in delight at being able to help her.

"You can summon up some anger too, I think." Alea looked up at Gar. "You may try to pretend that you don't have the ghost of an emotion, but I know better."

"You won't leave me in the shade," Gar assured her. "I do have a well of bitterness I can tap, and I've had some experience with madmen."

Alea looked at him again, startled, but he only said, "Lead on."

She turned away toward the city and started the long climb down.

14

The first houses they came to were burned out and gutted, roofs fallen in. Each was surrounded by dozens of leafless trunks, most with very few branches, many rotted and falling apart, all rising out of dry brown tangles of undergrowth—yards that had been overgrown until everything died. The street was choked with rubble and filled with potholes.

"However this city fell," Alea said, "it didn't just rot away quietly."

"It may not have gone out with one single bang, but it looks to have been noisy," Gar agreed. "Walk warily. Anything could be hiding in these hulks."

They went down along the cracked and pitted road as quickly as they could without running, trying to keep an eye on all four directions at once.

"Someone's watching me," Mira said, her face grim.

"I feel it, too," Blaize agreed.

"We knew they would," Gar said. "The only question is whether the watchers are alive or dead."

"Either way, they'll wait until we're too far in to be able to run," Alea guessed.

"So long as they chase away the soldiers," Gar said. "Blaize, how many ghosts are watching us?"

"Too many to count," the lad said, shivering. "Most of them seem sane, at least, but there are one or two whose minds are whirlpools of confusion."

"Don't let them drag you down," Gar advised. "Just note them in passing. Go quickly, friends—I don't think we've anything to fear until we come to the city's center."

The houses grew bigger as they marched eastward until they weren't houses anymore but tall buildings—taller and taller as they went, until Mira, Blaize, and Alea gaped at the towers around them. Gar contented himself with quick glances—compared to the palaces of Maxima and the clamoring mazes of Ceres City, this wasn't terribly impressive. "There's not a lot of light," he commented.

"No, these towers shut out the stars," Alea agreed. "We could kindle a torch."

"Here, let me," said a lugubrious voice beside them, and ghost-light flared in the darkness, bathing their faces in its blue-white glow.

The two younger folk leaped back with shouts of fright. Gar and Alea stiffened, drawing together without realizing it, glaring up at the native who towered above them, giggling in basso tones. He wore the robes of a guru and held up a forefinger whose nail blazed in a tongue of flame.

"Welcome to the city of Charenton," he said. "Welcome to the city of the mad."

Then he floated there giggling while the companions gaped up at him.

Gar was the first to recover. "Thank you for your hospitality.

Can you tell us if our enemies have followed us into the city?"

The ghost's brows pulled together, but his lips kept their smile as he lifted his head to gaze out along the boulevard down which they had come. "No, they've turned away, as anyone in his right mind would. Their masters aren't happy about it—shaking their fists at us and cursing—but they're turning back, too."

"Reasoning that we're out of their way, if we've come in here." Gar nodded. "I expect they'll be surprised when they find we've come out."

"Oh, I wouldn't say that," the ghost chuckled.

"Really?" Gar raised his eyebrows. "You don't think they expect us to return from a city, do you?"

"Of course they don't, and neither do I." The ghost blew out the flame on his finger.

With a racket of groans, howls, and clanking chains, half a dozen ghosts surrounded them, each twelve feet tall and bending down to reach for them with claw-tipped fingers.

Gar froze, and Alea rocked back against his chest while Blaize flung his arms around Mira and pressed his back against theirs. Then Alea recovered, glaring up at the guru's ghost.

With a scream of agony, he clapped his hands to his head.

Blaize saw and remembered that he was a ghost-leader. He turned a cold gaze on the nearest specter, a dapper gentleman in doublet and hose with a very nasty grin—which disappeared as his mouth formed an O of surprise before he doubled over, hands clawing at the pain in his belly.

Alea turned to look daggers at a hatchet-faced matron in full skirts and fuller bodice. The hatchet dulled amazingly as the woman clutched at her chest, eyes wide in panic, mouth gaping in wordless horror.

Blaize switched his gaze to a foppish ghost in a tailcoat, waistcoat, tight trousers with flaring cuffs, and a look of supercilious glee that turned to horror as he clutched at his throat, his howl choking off.

"Away!" cried the ghost of a young soldier, and all six specters vanished.

Blaize let out a sigh of relief and sagged. Mira looked up at him in alarm, then suddenly realized she was in his arms and twisted free. She caught his elbow and hauled upward. "Stand straight! They might come back—and they're surely watching!"

"Yes, pull yourself together." Alea didn't look much better but managed to stand straight and tall. "Mira's right, they're still here, even if they lack the courage to show themselves."

"Courage?" a new voice hooted, and a glowing gentleman in top hat and tails danced in the air before them. "Come now! What need have ghosts for courage? None can hurt us!"

"We just did," Alea reminded him. "Ask your friends."

"Oh, I was watching. Foolish creatures, to let you convince them they could feel pain."

"You, of course, know better?" Gar asked.

"Certainly! I'm Corbin the Magician! Look, Ma, no hands!" He held them, up white-gloved and fingers spread—just long enough for the companions to watch them disappear, leaving wrists and arms. "Look, Ma, no head!" Corbin cried, and sure enough, his head disappeared, too.

"Magician? Or conjurer?" Gar asked Alea.

"I conjure your head to come back!" Alea cried.

With a pop, the head reappeared atop Corbin's neck—without its top hat and saying indignantly, "I wasn't ready for that. Really, intruding on a gentleman when he isn't dressed!" With another pop, the top hat reappeared.

"We're wise to that trick," Alea informed him.

"Oh, yes, but not wise enough to fear us."

"What's to fear?" Gar asked. "The dead can't hurt the living, after all."

"Perhaps not truly hurt," the ghost said, "but there's pain, and then there's pain."

Suddenly the world seemed to spin around them. The towers seemed to lean—farther and farther, until they were about to fall, revealing a bulbous moon the color of blood. Indeed, it must have been blood, because it began to drip.

"He's mad," Blaize gasped, "and trying to make us mad with him! This is how he sees the world, as a confusing and threatening place!"

"Surely you know better now that you're dead!" Gar reproved—but he had to hold on to Alea to keep himself stable.

"Do I? Take a closer look." The ghost yanked his head off his shoulders and held it out, only a foot from Gar's face. The lips still moved as he spoke. "It's even more confusing now— you never know what might happen."

"That's no reason to lose your head." Gar stared into the ghost's empty eyes—and suddenly they disappeared, along with the rest of the head. From somewhere its mouth screeched, "What have you done? Where have you sent it?"

"If I send your body after it," Gar asked, "will you stay gone?"

"Never, vile fellow! I'll find it! It must be around here somewhere!" The ghost's arms flew off, sailing all about, feeling and palping. One hand brushed Mira's cheek; she shrieked and recoiled.

"You'll make a fellow feel unwanted!" the ghost protested. "Any head will do, after all. I'll try yours!"

Both hands converged on Mira. She screamed in utter panic.

"He can't really hurt you!" Blaize cried, and pushed her aside just in time for the hands to clasp his own temples. "I feel only a chill. Can't you find a better way to get a head in the afterworld?"

"The toe of my boot to you!" the unseen head cried, and

sure enough, the toe of one of his feet shot off arrowing toward Blaize.

"Go back where you came from," Blaize told it sternly, and the toe swung in a loop that sent it back toward its body.

"I have to hand it to you." One of the ghost's arms yanked the hand off the other and presented it to Blaize.

Mira shrieked and pressed against Alea.

"No, I'll give you a leg up," Blaize retorted. The ghost's right leg shot toward the sky, sending him flat on his back—or it would have if it had stayed attached. It yanked itself loose instead, and came swinging toward Blaize's face as the unseen head sang, "That's a poor way to get your kicks!"

"You heel!" Blaize said with disgust. "How low can you sink?" Sure enough, the foot shot toward the ground—and into it.

"How can a fellow make sense out of the world piecemeal?" the ghost protested.

"Oh, pull yourself together!" Alea said, exasperated, and all the parts of the specter shot back toward his torso and reattached themselves. A fuzzy ball appeared in the crook of his arm, shrinking in on itself and hardening into his head, leering out at them. "Well, I appreciate the help," it said, "but don't expect me to feel beholden."

"I don't expect you to feel anything in the state you're in," Alea retorted. "Just remember that we can take you apart and put you back together again."

"I'll remember you," the head sang, "if you dismember me."

"All right, if you wish." Alea stepped forward, rolling up her sleeves.

"No, no! I believe you! Just let me get my head on straight." The ghost took its head in its hands and screwed it back onto its shoulders. "Ah! That's better. All right, you've convinced me that you'll go where you will—but where will you go?"

"Back out of this city," Gar told him, "as soon as we're sure our pursuers have left."

"Pursuant to the all-clear? But till then, let me introduce you to some fascinating people! Bowles! Spenser! Solutre!"

They stepped from the shadows, lean men and women in ragged tunics and patched hose, the redhead on the left with a gloating grin and a crossbow leveled, the grizzled woman on the right giggling as she raised the nozzle of a flamethrower. In the center came a man as tall as Gar but as lean as a rail, seeming to be made of sticks and straw—his hair was even the pale, pale blond of new hay. His eyes alone seemed truly sane. Light winked on the whetted edge of the three-foot sword he carried before him.

Twenty more like them loomed out of the shadows, each with a wyvern on its shoulder. Some limped, one had a twisted foot, another a greatly enlarged shoulder, a third a harelip. Two advanced with the vacant eyes and slack smiles of the very simple, but they held their crossbows steady.

"You may have nothing to fear from ghosts," Corbin said, "but what about our descendants, and the outcasts who have sought sanctuary among us?"

Gar surveyed the approaching mob while Alea gathered herself, hand on the knife beneath her bodice, concentrating on mayhem. Gar called out, "Were you all born here, or are there some who came fleeing a cruel lord or the disgust of your fellows?"

The mob ground to a halt, the scarecrow in front frowning. "Some of us know what it is to flee," he said, "but don't think you can cozen us with that! This is our city and our district of it, and any who come must bow to us!"

"Don't you welcome fellow fugitives?" Gar asked.

"Aye, if they can pull their own weight and know their places!"

"Our place is out of here," Alea said. "Surely you won't insist on keeping us if you don't want us!"

"No, but we might have fun with you first." The grizzled woman pointed the nozzle of her flamethrower at Gar and giggled again.

"Are you a magician then, to play with fire?" Gar asked.

"We don't recognize that nonsense about magicians here," Corbin said with a laugh. "Everyone has some talent, large or small—but the tricks that are only tools and toys, why, I've taught that to them all."

"How many flamethrowers did you find?" Gar asked.

"Only a dozen." Corbin seemed mildly impressed by the term. "But they made a dozen more from spare parts."

"We've something of that knack ourselves," Gar told him. "Mira, show them your pets."

Mira straightened as though coming out of a daze, then smiled and raised her arms, crying out with a cawing noise. The wyverns sprang from the warriors' shoulders and streaked toward her, one landing on her outstretched leather-clothed arm, the others perching on stone ledges as close to her as they could get, hissing and cooing. Their owners cried out in indignation.

"Give us back our wyverns!" cried a voice from the crowd, and a red-faced man stepped forward. He was dressed like the others and, like them, sprouted the sores of vitamin deficiencies, but he stretched out an arm, making a noise halfway between a coo and a caw, and two of the wyverns leaped into the air to shoot back to land on his shoulder and forearm.

"Come, the rest of you!" he said sternly.

Mira stroked the scaly head and sinuous neck of the wyvern on her arm; it closed its eyes in pleasure. "You can trust them with me."

"Trust you to turn them against us, aye! Give them back, or I'll loose my human friends!"

"I'd hate to have these pretty fliers torn between the two of us," Mira said sadly. "Can't you believe their opinion of me?"

The wyverneer glowered at her and her new pet, then reluctantly allowed, "Aye, that I can. How are you bewitching them, anyway? It's taken me a year to learn to drive that one!"

"I don't drive them," Mira told him. "I flatter and befriend them. They come to me for pleasure, not out of fear."

"Spoiling them rotten, I'll warrant," the wyverneer said in disgust. "Still, I'll trust their opinion. If they say you're good, I'll believe them. My name's Stukely."

"Mine is Mira," she said, eyes wide in surprise.

"Well, if she's trustworthy, maybe the rest of you are," said the tall skeletal man. "I'm Longshanks." He transferred the sword to his left hand and held out his right.

Gar took it, though his own left hand still rested on his dagger. "I'm Gar Pike."

"Gar, are you?" Longshanks grinned. "Seems we're named alike."

"I'm Solutre." The grizzled woman reached out to Alea. "I know I'm gruff, but someone has to keep these lugs in line."

"I know what you mean," Alea said with a smile as she clasped the woman's hand.

Gar looked at her askance but said nothing.

"And who have we here?" The redhead advanced on Blaize. "What can you do for your friends, fellow?" He frowned as Blaize shrank away. "What's the matter? Think I've got the plague?"

"I—I've heard the rumors."

The redhead laughed. "What, that we're all diseased maniacs?"

"That, and that every one of you is a witch and has a familiar in the form of a wyvern."

There was a moment of silence. Then the warriors exploded into laughter, their weapons drooping.

"Well, that's a new twist on the old lies," the redhead said, grinning. "Most of us do have pets, but they're real wyverns, my lad, not demons. As to witchcraft, why, what's the difference between that and a lord's magic, I'd like to know?"

"Magic—magic follows rules," Blaize stammered. "Witchcraft breaks them all and intends evil."

"Oh, and the magicians only use their powers for healing and helping? Pull the other one, fellow! We've the same sorts of power as the lords, only we don't think of it as magic! That lass with you, now, she has a way with animals, nothing more."

"So . . . you're not witches?" Blaize asked.

"Not a bit," the redhead assured him. He called to his fellows, "Any of you have dealings with devils, mates?"

They all shook their heads with a chorus of denial, some amazed at the idea, some angry, most amused.

"So unless you've made a pact with a devil yourself, there are no witches here," the redhead said. "I'm Bowles, by the way. Who're you?"

"B-Blaize is my name."

"Well enough then, B-Blaize," Bowles mimicked. "What good are you, though? Do your friends just carry you along out of kindness?"

"Of course not!"

"What can you do, then?"

"Why, bring friends of my own," Blaize answered. "They're right here, waiting to see if I'll need them."

"Oh, are they indeed," the redhead scoffed. "Tell them to show themselves and I'll believe you."

"Why wait?" asked a voice.

Bowles spun about to see Conn towering over him, glowing and glowering.

"Just say the word, Blaize," said a voice behind Bowles. He spun about to see Ranulf leaning down with a genial grin and a spectral saber, its point at the man's throat.

"Here, now! That's my great-great-grandson!" Corbin cried, affronted. "Just because you died too soon to father a child is no reason to be jealous!"

"Oh, I fathered one, all right." Ranulf cast the conjurer a quick glance. "I just didn't get to stick around to watch him grow up—well, not in the flesh, anyway."

"A ghost father's better than none," Conn protested.

"Yes, but not much, is he?" Ranulf said sourly. "He can't play ball with you, after all. But my boy and girl did develop amazing imaginations."

"How did you know we were coming?" Gar asked.

"Why, we heard your thoughts, of course!" Longshanks grinned. "Didn't think you were the only one who could tell what a man was thinking, did you?"

"I can, but I usually don't," Gar said. "That doesn't mean I won't listen, of course,"

"Of course," Longshanks agreed.

"Mind you, I'm always glad to make new friends," Alea said warily, "but what made you decide we were all right so quickly?"

"Well, partly the wyverns liking your young friend there," Longshanks said judiciously, "and partly that we can hear your thoughts and don't find any malice in them . . ."

". . . but chiefly that you were able to take all my teasing and toss it right back at me," Corbin said.

"Well, it means we wouldn't want to fight you if we didn't have to, anyway," Longshanks said with a grin. "Come share a meal with us, if you think you can trust us."

They found the rest of the clan in an overgrown park surrounded on four sides by blank-faced, empty-windowed ruins of buildings. The ragtag horde was gathered around a central campfire in the plasticrete ring of what had once been a goldfish pond. They were dressed in tunics, hoses, blouses, and skirts dyed in bright colors. Alea wondered where they had found the dyes. They hailed the newcomers cheerfully. Walking among them, under trees with varicolored leaves that none of the companions had ever seen before, Alea saw deformities of all sorts, as well as the wild or distracted eyes of madness and the vacant gazes of mental retardation—but most seemed quite sane, and many weren't deformed at all, though they bore the scars of their lords' cruelty. Runaways they were, like Mira and Blaize, but few seemed bitter and all seemed cheerful, even happy. Alea marveled that the outcasts had made a home.

Over meat—they didn't ask what kind—the bragging contest began. It started with a question—innocent enough in its way, if you took it as it was intended. Longshanks looked straight at Gar and asked, "Are you a madman, a criminal, or a runaway?"

Gar stared, then smiled and asked, "Do I have to be one of the three?"

"No one else comes to the cities," Solutre told him. "They're afraid of the ghosts—and us. They're right to be, too."

"Are you so powerful a group of warriors as that?"

"We have to be, to hold our own against the Hawks and the Hounds," Bowles said.

Gar frowned. "What are the Hawks and the Hounds?"

Bowles peered closely at him. "You really don't read minds unless you have to, do you?"

"Uncommonly polite," Longshanks noted.

"I can't listen to every thought that comes by or I'd go crazy," Gar said.

The others looked up, startled.

Gar decided that it took some effort for them to read minds.

Even then, they could probably only hear thoughts that were put into words or pictures. "Well, think of the Hawks and the Hounds and I'll see them in your mind."

"No need," Bowles said quickly. "They're the tribes that border us on each side of our wedge."

"Wedge?" Gar asked.

"The road we followed came straight from the edge of the city," Alea told him. "It probably goes straight through to the center of town. If there are more radial roads like that, the whole city's cut up into . . . what? Eight wedges? Twelve?" she asked Bowles.

"Six," he told her, "and we have to keep the Hawks and the Hounds away from our game if we want to have enough to eat."

"Game?" Gar asked. "Are there animals in this city?"

"You'd be surprised how they came in and multiplied once the magic juice stopped flowing through the wires and the city died," Longshanks said grimly. "Come hunt with us and see for yourself. What weapons can you use?"

"Weapons?" Gar asked. "Well, we all carry daggers and staves."

"Won't do much good against a dog pack," Solutre opined. "Can any of you use a sling?"

"I can," Gar and Blaize said together, then looked at one another in surprise.

"Take these, then." Solutre handed them each a leather cup with thongs wrapped about it. "Spenser, fetch spears for these two! Just think of it as a staff with a point on the end," she told Mira and Alea.

Spenser was a hard-faced woman who looked to be in her thirties, which in a hardscrabble society like this probably meant she was about twenty-five. She gave each of the women a spear. Thus armed, and with half the people in the party accompanied by rangy knee-high lop-eared mongrels with tan fur, long muzzles, and curving tails, they set off to see what kind of game a concrete forest could hold.

It had trees, for one thing, some in odd places. Wherever dead leaves had drifted and rotted to make humus, seeds had caught, sprouted, and, in growing, split the pavement. Even more, the wedge had apparently been laid out with a little park every few blocks; each had developed an orchard.

"Hold on—let's see what's ripe," Solutre said.

"Ward!" Longshanks snapped. He, Bowles, Spenser, and half a dozen others took up their stations with bows and spears on two sides of the little park, the other two walls being buildings. Some ancestor, with knowledge and cunning, had espaliered fruit trees against those walls, and a dozen trees filled the square. Between the grove and the walls stood a stand of maize. Solutre inspected it, seeming satisfied. "Most of the ears have set on," she told Alea.

"So you're farming, too," Alea said.

"In a small way," Solutre said. "We can't exactly clear— Watch out!"

Something pink and bulbous came charging out of the stalks. Alea leaped aside, sweeping the point of the spear by reflex. The hog squealed in rage and turned on her, but an arrow buried itself in the animal's side, and it stumbled, then fell. Alea turned away and left Solutre to finish the beast.

"We'll eat well tonight," the woman said.

Alea turned back and saw her sheathing a knife as a young man tied the hog's hooves together and shoved a spear through to carry it. Solutre inspected the animal's belly. "A sow, right enough, but not nursing. Too bad—we could have used a few more in the pen."

"How . . . how did pigs come into this city?" Alea asked.

"Our ancestors tell us some folks had started keeping them as pets," Solutre told her, "a special breed, pretty little things that never grew much hair or got to be any bigger than knee-high. When the crash came, they started running loose and bred back to your average wild pig."

Alea looked at the sow slung between the shoulders of a young man and a young woman. Its back had stood halfway up her thigh, and it was covered with mottled black and white hair. "A far cry from a pet indeed."

"So are we," Solutre grunted.

When the sun slipped below the tallest buildings, they started back. Every structure they passed had the lowest two stories of windows boarded up, even if the higher ones lacked glass. The doors were stout and locked. Alea wondered why.

They hadn't gone more than a few blocks through the ruins when she found out. They were going down a wide street, laughing and chatting as they detoured around rusted hulks of vehicles and piles of fallen brick and stone, when they head a deep, hollow sound. Instantly they stilled. The sound came again, and Longshanks said in a tense whisper, "Listen for thoughts, Solutre."

They were silent a moment. Then, "Hawks!" Solutre hissed.

15

Instantly the whole party stilled. The carriers laid down the pig and took up their bows. Some nocked arrows to their strings, others set small rocks in their slings. Spear carriers slanted their weapons to guard.

The baffling thing was that there was no one in sight. As silently as the ancestral ghosts who had trained them, the band glided over broken pavement and around the corner.

A dozen people very much like them, in almost identical tunics and hose but with their hair combed high and stiffened into crests, stood around one of the doors while two of their number struck it with axes.

"Corbies!" one of them shouted.

The axe wielders turned, brandishing tools suddenly become weapons. Others drew their bows. One or two even had a sword.

"What do you think you're doing, coming into our wedge like this?" Longshanks yelled, striding toward them. "Trying to break into one of our buildings! Do we come sneaking into your alleys? Do we try to chop down your doors?"

"Yes!" shouted a squat, broad man who looked to be all

muscle. He waddled forward, bullet head thrust out pugnaciously. "So we come marching into your boulevards, right out in the open, no sneaking for us! What if we do? What's so precious you keep it locked up?"

"Jewels and gold! Silver candlesticks and plates!" Longshanks boasted from behind his sword as he went nearer, a step at a time. "But you can't have them, not an ounce! They're ours and only ours!"

"Only your imagination, you mean!" the broad man hooted. "If you've so much finery, open your door and show us!"

"If I opened my door as much as you open your mouth, I might as well throw it away, for it would never be shut!"

As Gar, Alea, Blaize and Mira watched, amazed, the two bands shouted insult after insult at one another, the Corbies edging closer, the Hawks retreating a step at a time, until finally, with much growling and shaking of weapons, the Hawks departed, withdrawing across the boulevard and into the leaves of what was, presumably, a park of their own.

"Well, that's why we patrol the borders every day," Solutre told Alea. "If we'd let them get into that building, it would have cost blood and lives to get them out."

It was very clear to Alea that only good luck had brought the band in time to prevent just that. "Weren't you worried that they might have started shooting?"

"If they'd loosed arrows, so would we," Solutre said grimly. "Now and again we find a building opened like that, so we lie in wait and make sure they're not coming out again. If they don't, we track them to their border and leave them a sign to tell them we're on to their tricks."

"What if they do come out while you're there?" Mira asked, troubled.

"Then we fight," Solutre boasted, "until they run like the cowards they are, run the way they did today!"

Alea hadn't seen any running, but she hadn't seen any blood spilled either. "I'm glad it works," she said, feeling numb.

"Works right well, and you'd better believe it!" Solutre shook her bow for emphasis. "They don't want fighting with the Corbies because they don't want to have to bury the ones who would die! A band needs every member it's got!"

Alea reflected that was surely true of the Corbies themselves, too.

She went for a walk with her companion, while dinner was cooking.

"Can they fight as well as they claim?" she wondered.

"If they can fight at all," Mira said with conviction, "they're far better off than we serfs!"

"There's truth in that, I'll wager," Gar said thoughtfully, "and they do seem to be trained in the use of weapons, even if they never use them against other people."

Alea gave him a quick and incisive glance. "You're planning to use them yourself!"

"Why, no," Gar said equably, "only to let them use us—or our knowledge, at least."

So after supper, he and Alea went apart, but still well within sight of the band, and sat down to meditate. It only took fifteen minutes before Solutre came over to Mira and demanded, "What are they doing, just sitting there like that?"

"Meditating," Mira told her.

"Meditating?" Solutre said in disbelief. "What kind of magic is that?"

"Only concentration," Mira said. "They're trying to understand how everything fits together. It's sort of like dreaming when you're awake."

Solutre could see the sense in that. She watched Gar and

Alea, her face thoughtful. Then she went and spoke with some of her clansfolk, who also turned thoughtful.

Mira turned to Blaize, amused. "How long do you think it will be before they're pestering Gar and Alea to teach them?"

"Tomorrow." Blaize glanced around at their hosts. "They pride themselves on their magic, even though they pretend there is no such thing. I don't mind telling you, I won't sleep easily tonight."

Mira stared at him, feeling his apprehension; it awakened fears she had been trying to quell. "But they seem so ordinary, once you look past the oddness of their bodies and hair and ornaments! Surely they can't really be the monsters of the old wives' tales!"

"I wouldn't think so, but they've had so many surprises for us already," Blaize said. "I can't get those old stories out of my mind, that the cities held only diseased madmen whose mere touch would infect you with a horrible illness!"

Mira shivered at the memory of just such a tale but said, stoutly, "Well, they haven't tried to touch us yet—and as to their being mad, I've seen a few whose eyes are too bright and whose laughs are too shrill, but most of them seem as sane as a magician's guard."

"They seem so, yes." But Blaize's doubt was almost palpable. "I don't see much evidence of disease, though."

"Maybe the sick ones died out," Mira offered.

"That would make sense," Blaize agreed. He glanced over at the band around the fire pit, laughing and joking now at the end of the day. Several young couples were holding hands. "They're as hard-handed and muscular as any serfs," Blaize mused, "but there's a dignity about them, an assurance that I don't remember from my village."

"They're free," Mira said, her voice low. "That's the difference."

"It comes at a price, though," Blaize said thoughtfully. "They can't be sure there will be enough game to keep them fed from one day to the next."

Mira shrugged. "What happens to the serfs when there's a drought?"

"Famine," Blaize said, his voice flat. "The lords still have enough, but the serfs starve. Maybe these folks don't have it so badly after all."

"And they have a home." Mira's eyes filled with longing. "A home, and people to help them if they need it, and defend them if they need that, too."

Blaize felt the echo of her yearning within him. He'd had two homes, one with his parents and one with Arnogle, and he missed them both very strongly.

Dawn saw a dozen city people sitting in a circle with Gar and Alea. Within a week, the two had taught them the basics of Taoism and they were beginning to wonder about their intermittent strife with the Hawks and the Hounds. But they were shocked when a Hawk party came into their home block carrying a flag of truce.

Longshanks went forward to meet them with half a dozen heavily armed warriors. "Good hunting to you," he said warily.

"And to you," the Hawk speaker said. "May the game in your wedge multiply."

"And in yours." Longshanks forced a smile. "What's the occasion for this chat? Not that it's unpleasant, mind you, only surprising."

"Well . . . ah . . . we've heard you have some shamans visiting, who are teaching you wisdom. We'd like to share it, if we may."

"They call themselves sages, not shamans." Longshanks frowned. "Who told you of them?"

"Our ancestors."

There was nothing else to wonder about—they all knew that ghosts talked to ghosts. There was some discussion as to whether or not Gar and Alea were willing to go, but since they were, Longshanks tried to put Taoism into practice by exchanging gifts with the Hawks, then the companions go teach.

The Hawks learned as quickly as the Corbies. At the end of the week, they proved it by inviting their neighbors to a banquet. Corbin told his descendants to go bearing gifts, and with double game to roast, the two tribes had a high old time of it.

The next day, the Hounds sent emissaries to ask the teachers to visit. By the end of the month, Gar and Alea had visited each of the six tribes, and all were beginning their days with meditation and trying to find ways to practice Taoism in their daily lives, including martial arts practice. The feuding stopped, but they weren't quite ready for Gar's suggestion that they merge their clan meetings into a citywide council.

Gar was positively ecstatic. "Success beyond my wildest hopes!" he told Alea. "I never dreamed they could learn so quickly!"

"They've been wanting to find a way to end the fighting for a long time," Alea answered, "and the meditation is strengthening the powers that they say they don't have."

That night, she couldn't sleep. Feeling restless, she wandered off into the concrete canyons by herself. Somehow she forgot that it might be dangerous.

Then she turned a corner and met a giant globe of a cathead with a toothy grin and an afterthought of a body.

"I might have known it would be you!" Alea jammed her fists on her hips. "Why don't you let me remember these meetings? It would make my work a great deal easier!"

"You're doing quite well remembering the ideas we discuss," Evanescent said easily. "No need to remember where you found them."

"And what ideas am I 'finding' tonight?"

"The cure to this planet's problems," Evanescent told her. "There are enough of these city people to beat the magicians' guards. They even have the combined psi power to muzzle the magicians themselves."

"I don't like the idea of starting a war," Alea said darkly.

"You won't be," Evanescent assured her. "Some ghost told the magicians about you. They're horrified at the idea of the city barbarians uniting. They're already on the march—ten magicians with five hundred guards."

Alea felt a chill, one that was swamped by the heat of anger. "That ghost wouldn't have had the idea from you, would he?"

"My dear!" Evanescent said in wounded tones. "How could you think I would even consider such a thing? Besides, I didn't have to—the ghost was a power-hungry shaman who tried to make this whole city his own little kingdom during the Collapse. He's outraged to see the barbarians unifying without a lord."

"So he's bringing in lords to divide them up?"

"Yes, but I'm sure your clans can fight them off. Don't worry, dear, I'll help. You can be sure the magicians' magic won't work very well."

Alea looked down, frowning in thought, then looked up at the empty courtyard, wondering how the broken fountain could still be spouting water—an artesian well, no doubt. Like the human spirit, it welled up again and again, even in the midst of the ruins.

Well, the spirit of these barbarians wouldn't be ruined, she would see to that. She went back to the empty lobby the Corbies had assigned herself and her companions as sleeping quarters. She wondered if she should wake Gar with this galvanizing news or wait till morning.

She decided to wait.

• • •

They were wakened by angry shouts and the clatter of shields and spears being taken up. With a sinking stomach, she knew she shouldn't have waited.

"What is it?" Gar sat up, blinking sleep out of his eyes.

"The alarm." Alea scrambled up. "The magicians are marching on the city. Quickly! We've got to remind the Corbies about the Way! They're forgetting it completely and going back to their old mob fighting!"

Gar grabbed his clothes, stuffed his long body into them, and ran out into the street.

Blaize and Mira looked up blinking and confused.

"Call every wyvern you've got!" Alea told Mira, and to Blaize, "Organize the ghosts and tell them to look for traitors! Maybe they can't hurt one another, but they can keep the enemy's phantoms busy!"

They dashed out. Alea was right behind them, completely unafraid of the magicians.

The barbarians were another matter, though. They could lose by sheer lack of discipline—but Gar was already there, calling, wheedling, cajoling. "Remember the Way! Don't attack them—make them come to you! Use their own violence against them!"

"Nice phrases," Longshanks scoffed. "How do you do it?"

"This is your land, your terrain," Gar told him. "You know where to hide, how to appear and disappear. Show yourselves long enough to make them chase you, bait them into a courtyard, and trap them there. Lead them down a narrow street where you have people at the windows with rocks to throw. Entice them down into cellars, lock the doors, and station guards to keep them in. Don't kill them if you don't have to—when we let them go and chase them out, we want them spreading the word that you're merciful as well as unbeatable."

Longshanks stared at him, startled. Then he turned to Solutre with a grin.

The invasion was a disaster—for the invaders. With their lords threatening and blustering, they came marching down a rubble-strewn avenue, but they eyed the buildings to either side with great trepidation shaking in their boots.

"Cowards! Poltroons!" shouted one magician, following behind his troops. He shook a fist at the empty window to either side of him. "Come out and show yourselves! You can't hide from us forever!"

Half a dozen bowmen ducked from behind a corner and loosed a flight of arrows. A sergeant saw them and shouted, "Shields up!" The soldiers obeyed and were rewarded with the sounds of arrows thudding into wood and leather.

"See?" the sergeant bellowed. "They can't hurt you! After them!"

The soldiers cheered and charged.

Around the corner they went, just in time to see the last of the bowmen ducking through a hole in a wall. "There they go!" the sergeant shouted, pointing.

"What's on the other side of that wall?" a guard asked nervously.

"Nothing, you fool! Can't you see the daylight? It's just a shortcut—they were too lazy to go around, so they knocked a hole in it! Come on, men!"

The troopers whooped and ran after him.

Through the hole they charged—then skidded to a halt as they saw the blank wall ahead of them. Whirling, they saw a wall on each side, too. They turned back to the hole—and found it filled with bowmen, arrows leveled. Each had a wyvern on his shoulder.

"Lay down your arms and we'll let you live." The leader's grin held a hint of madness. "Don't think you have a choice, either. Look up."

"Not all of us!" the sergeant kept his glare on the bowmen. "Roark, tell me what you see!"

"Windows, Sergeant," the trooper said nervously, "way up high, and every one has a madman with a sling."

"We're not mad!" the leader snapped. "We do have some odd talents, though. Lay down your arms, or we'll loose our pets—and call in our ancestors."

The troopers shuddered but the sergeant chose bluster. "We've a magician lord only a step behind us, and he'll make your wyverns into fireballs if you dare loose them!"

"Your lord has his hands full at the moment," the spokesman said with a gloating smile. "He's fighting the ghosts of three magicians who have been dead a hundred years—and learning more about magic every day. You're on your own, lads."

A rock clattered on the tiles of the courtyard. The soldier nearest shied away.

"Stop that!" the leader called sharply. "We're still giving them the chance to surrender!"

"We surrender, we surrender!" the sergeant declared in disgust. He threw down his pike. His troopers imitated him on the instant and the courtyard filled with the clatter of falling arms.

"Kick them over here," the bowman said.

The soldiers kicked their pikes and halberds into a pile near the hole in the wall.

"Good. Now back away."

They did, and a couple of city dwellers ducked in through the hole, gathered up the weapons, and carried them out.

"This is your prison now," the bowman said. "Don't try to get out until we tell you. Your guards will be watching you with stones to hand. You won't see them, but they'll be there."

For emphasis, a stone cracked into the pavement two yards in front of the sergeant. It bounced several times. He saw how it had split the flagstone.

The bowmen stepped back and a rusty iron grid slid over the hole in the wall—obviously two old gates welded together.

"It might be weak," Roark muttered in the sergeant's ear. "We might be able to break it."

A stone whizzed through the air and struck one of the bars.

Roark shivered. "Those boys throw straight."

"That one was a girl," the soldier behind him said. "Pretty ugly, too."

Roark glanced up to see for himself, but the window was empty.

"Don't think I want to take the chance of going near those bars," the sergeant said. "Too bad, boys—looks like we're here for the duration."

"Yeah, too bad." Roark sighed. "I'm really going to miss the scrimmage."

"Yeah, so am I," another trooper said happily. "Who's got the cards?"

Two streets away, another score of soldiers crouched under their shields while a constant stream of rocks rained down on them. Three of them were covering their magic-lord and wincing at the occasional pebble that bounced up to strike their shins.

"They have to run out of rocks sometime!" the sergeant called.

"No we don't!" a voice shrilled above him. "We've got whole buildings stuffed with stones!" It broke into an eerie laugh that echoed down the concrete canyon, joined by many other cackling voices.

A soldier shuddered. "It's bad enough being ambushed, but ambushed by madmen is worse!"

"Smite them with fire, my lord!" the sergeant implored.

"I can't!" the magician snapped. "Someone's dousing the flames as quickly as I start them."

The sergeant blinked. "Who?"

"I'm not sure he's alive anymore," the magician admitted.

All his men shuddered. One asked in a quaver, "What happens if we're still stuck here at night?"

"Lord Kraken will call ghosts of his own to match these!" the magician blustered.

The soldiers took that in silence, suspecting that there were a great many more city ghosts than the number Lord Kraken could call.

Suddenly the drumming of stones ceased.

The soldiers looked up, stupefied. Warily, the sergeant peeked out around the edge of his shield. Sure enough, the bombardment had stopped.

"We'll let you go," the shrill voice skirled, "if you march back the way you came and keep marching till you're home."

"And if we don't?" the magician called truculently.

"Then we'll keep you here till we need you."

"Need us?" The sergeant stared. "For what? And how long?"

"Until we run out of meat," the voice called back. "That won't take long—we can't hunt while we're pinning you here."

The soldiers put two and two together and shuddered.

"All right, we'll retreat!" the magician shouted. "But you'll regret this! I'll be back with five times this number!"

"We'll look forward to it," the voice called. "Bring plenty of food—you'll be here a while."

As dusk fell, the cellar window opened and a waterskin came flying through. The soldiers trapped inside caught it, blinking in surprise. "Thanks!" the sergeant called.

"We're nothing if not hospitable," a gruff voice answered. "Watch out for the food, now!"

The men jumped back as three huge sacks sailed in, one after another.

"You'll have to mix it with the water and bake it yourselves," the gruff voice growled. "Just build the fire close to the window so the smoke can get out."

"Uh . . . right . . ." the sergeant said. "How long you planning to keep us here?"

"As long as you want," the barbarian answered. "You can go anytime, as long as you go and don't come back."

"We can't," the sergeant said heavily. "Our lord won't let us."

"Oh, I think he'll be ready by morning," the barbarian answered. "He's arguing with our ancestors, and they have his ghosts outnumbered three to one already."

16

lready?" the sergeant asked in a hollow voice.

"There're more ghosts coming," the barbarian explained.

The sergeant shuddered and looked around the clammy cellar. All of a sudden it seemed very cozy.

All over the city, similar groups of soldiers were imprisoned or penned up one way or another. None of them struggled terribly hard to free themselves.

When morning came and their guards told them to go, they came out blinking, dazed, and calling for their magicians. No one answered and each squadron of troopers searched until they found their lord—dead. The ghost-handler's face was a rictus of horror; he had met more terrible phantoms than his own. The fire-handler's tank had clearly exploded. The master of wyverns had died with talons in his heart, and the earth-shaker lay buried under a pile of fallen masonry. The magician whose peasants had lived in fear of poisonous vapors and contaminated food lay twisted by internal agony.

Some silent and some openly rejoicing, the troops filed out of the city along the boulevard—most of them. One out of ten stayed behind. The sergeants later claimed they were missing in action, but they weren't fooling anybody. The troopers all knew that a dead lord meant only that a neighboring magician would commandeer his land and serfs. They had preferred to take their chances with the outcasts of the city ruins.

"We have some new pupils," Alea told Gar.

"I won't teach anybody who doesn't want to learn." Gar frowned at the fifty troopers in different liveries who stood more or less at attention, watching him anxiously.

"Oh, we want to," a sergeant assured him. "Anybody who can beat a magician so handily but find room to let the troopers live—well, whatever you've taught these city folk, we need to learn, too."

"It was the clans who showed you mercy," Alea pointed out.

"The mercy that you taught them, lady! You're not fooling anybody—everybody knows these city people used to spend most of their time fighting each other. Anybody who can convince them to stick together—well, maybe she knows something that can help the serfs."

Alea looked up at Gar with a bright smile. Slowly, he nodded.

The new recruits had been training for two weeks when Alea asked, over the clan's campfire one night, "What's happened to Conn and Ranulf? I haven't seen them for weeks."

"Bored, I expect," Gar said. "Their only reason for hanging around us was for amusement, after all."

A maniacal laugh rang through the courtyard. Everyone leaped up, but it was only Corbin materializing in middance and crying, "Get a good night's sleep and be up before the sun, people. You have another army coming."

"Another?" Longshanks rose with a scowl. "Who this time?"

"Ten more magicians, each with fifty guards. Most of the soldiers are green, though—fresh from the plow and scarcely trained at all."

"What we did to the last five hundred, we can do to five hundred more. Why do they march?"

"Oh, they've heard about you," Corbin told them. "The ghosts who came with that last batch didn't stick around, you know. They went back home and told the nearest magicians they could find. I gather some of them made it sound as though you're planning an assault, and if the magicians wait too long, you're going to explode out of your cities and conquer them all."

"What nonsense!" Solutre said indignantly. "All we ask is to be left alone in our exile as we always have been!"

"Well, you can't ask so little anymore," Corbin told her. "The magicians grilled the soldiers who came back and found out that most of what the ghosts said was true—that your tribes have united, that you're tougher fighters than any of the soldiers, and that every other one of you is a magician."

"None of us is a magician!"

"By your standards, no," Corbin acknowledged, "but by the standards of men who use the title to overawe the weak and ignorant, yes."

"We can't help what they call themselves," Solutre retorted.

"No, but we can show them up for what they are," Longshanks said grimly, "ordinary men who happen to have an extra talent each." He turned to the young folk. "Gawain, find that Hawk girl you're sweet on and tell her what's happening."

Gawain blushed as the other youngsters set up catcalls and jibes.

"Stop," Solutre said, not loudly, but they stopped. "There's no time for that," she explained.

"Axel, you go tell the Hounds," Longshanks directed. "Manon, that Fox boy you've been eyeing . . ."

Manon leaped to her feet and turned away, not quite quickly enough to hide the reddening of her cheeks.

"Ander, you go to the Elks," Longshanks directed. "Thall, you take the Badgers."

The youngsters nodded and dashed away.

"All right, we'll do as we did last time," Longshanks told his people, "but we can't use the same tricks—they'll have heard about them and be ready. Any ideas?"

"If they're coming with ghost-scouts, you'll have to get the specters out of the way first," Blaize said. "How about persuading the city ghosts to set up a clamor? When the soldiers start to charge toward it, their ghosts will speed ahead to see what it is, and your ancestors can hit them with a screaming match. That should scare the soldiers out of that street, and you can have decoys waiting."

"Good thought." Longshanks nodded. "What if they don't scare?"

"Have wyverns waiting in the buildings on either side," Mira suggested. "They can hit the soldiers so quickly that they won't have time to shoot down the darlings."

"Only a wyverneer could call her pets a darling," Solutre said drily, "but it's a good idea."

"There's that old foundation over on Third and Tenth that we covered up with boards," a broad man said. "We could pile rubble on it, shoot at the soldiers from it, and when they charge us, yank away the boards."

"Yes, and there's that rotten pier down by the river!" a matronly woman said, eyes alight. "We can send a few canoes down to shoot at them, and when they crowd onto the pier to shoot back, they'll end up in the water!"

Three others started to speak at once.

"I'm starting to feel left out," Alea told Gar.

"That's just fine," he replied, his face glowing.

She eyed him askance. "What are you so happy abut?"

"It's always a delight to see how well your students have learned," Gar said.

The sentries were on watch all night, but they didn't see anything until dawn.

"Three columns!" one called down from the highest building. Others on lower floors had to relay her cry down to street level. "They're coming in on the Boulevard of the Elysian Fields, the Linden Tree Promenade, and the Broad Way!"

"Trying to cut three wedges off from one another," Solutre grunted. "Don't the fools realize they'll have enemies to left and to right?"

"Probably do," Longshanks answered. "Won't do them much good, though. Bait the traps."

The soldiers came marching down the boulevards with their magicians right behind them, watching for stragglers who might try to desert—a wise precaution, from the fearful looks the raw recruits cast about them (and some of the veterans, too). Each troop had assigned a lookout for the sky, watching for stones dropping and wyverns swooping. Even so, the soldiers marched with their shields over their heads; only the first rank held theirs in front.

Longshanks watched from the shadows of a second-story window. "We'll do as we did last time—wait till they split up into search parties. Then we'll start leading them into the traps."

But these magicians had heard from the ghosts what had happened to their predecessors and kept their troops together: three magicians each on the Boulevard of the Elysian Fields and the Linden Tree Promenade, and four on the Broad Way, in the center. Their intermittent bickering showed their own nervousness—or perhaps only longstanding rivalries born of greed. When they did finally leave the boulevards, they left in a body.

"They're not going to let you divide and conquer," Alea said.

"No, they're not," Solutre agreed. "At least we can leave the outer two to the other four clans. These, though, are our meat—ours and the Hounds'."

On a terrace overlooking the Boulevard of the Elysian Fields, Gar stood beside Gyre, who led the Hawks as much as anyone did. "They're looking for your village," Gar told him.

"If you can call two floors of a building a village," Gyre said with a dry smile. "Well, we'd better give them something to find. Leiora! Take five people and go light a bonfire on top of the Ocre Building!"

A young woman nodded, tagged two other women and three men, and headed for the stairs.

"My lord! There, smoke!" A sergeant pointed.

"A village on top of a tower—I suppose it makes sense," Magician Lurby growled. "Well, if they can climb it, so can we!"

When they found the building, though, the soldiers stared up eighty stories, their stomachs sinking. "Did the ancients climb that high every day?" one asked.

"Not likely," Lord Lurby growled. "They lived there, worked there, and probably only came out once a month or so. Still, when they came back, they had to climb. Find a door."

They found a doorway closed by boards instead.

"Tear them down!" the magician ordered.

The boards came down easily, revealing a double door of glass and metal, both panels sagging and partly open, though the glass was intact.

"They don't guard their portal very well," Lurby sneered. "In and up!"

The soldiers burst through the doors and found no one in the cavern except the bright mosaics and metal strips inlaid on the walls. They prowled about, past the strange recessed panels with rows of numbers above them, and finally found a stairway behind a deceptively modest door.

"Beware ambush," the sergeant warned. "Only one at a time can file through there. Five men could hold it against an army."

But there were no enemies on the other side. In they went and started climbing, two hundred men two abreast, tense and wary, expecting a squadron of defenders around every turn— but they found none. They climbed.

And climbed. And climbed.

As they mounted on the north side of the building, Leiora and her five friends slipped down the stairway on the far side, leaving their bonfire burning atop the elevator shaft.

By the time the magicians and their forces reached the top, it was night and the fire only embers. When they found the roof floor empty, they were too tired to curse.

"Foolish notion, to go trying to climb a tower such as this!" Magician Stour barked at Lurby.

"Then why didn't you say so before we started?" Lurby snarled.

"We came up because we thought they had a village here," Korkand the wyverneer said, exasperated. "We were all keen for the hunt. Well, at least my wyverns can find us a way down. Still, I'd rather they do the climbing, not me."

They were too weary to bicker further, but a good night's sleep would remedy that.

The magicians Lurk, Goth, Vis, and Ghouri the Ghost-Caller marched down the Broad Way until they came to the first of the towers. There they split their force in two, one hundred to the west, one hundred to the east, not realizing that each half of the army was scouting the territory of a different barbarian band—Lurk and Goth to the Hounds' territory, Ghouri and Vis to the Corbies'.

"They're off the Broad Way!" Longshanks slapped the terrace rail in triumph. "Now to lead them astray!"

"Why bother leading them?" Alea asked. "Remember the Way and let them search. Just pull your people back out of their way."

"Yes, Longshanks," Solutre said with a grin. "What flatlander can find his way among our towers, after all?"

Sure enough, they couldn't. Ghouri even called up the neighborhood ghosts, who helpfully gave him directions that led him around in a four-hour circle. Finally tumbling to their ruse, he asked his own ghosts for guidance, but they had to search, and the city ancestors kept interrupting them with jibes and jeers, destroying their concentration and confusing them completely. Around and around they went through mazes of city streets until, weary and confused, Ghouri and Vis bade their men pitch camp in one of the city's squares, where seeds had taken root between slabs of plasticrete and, by growing, broken them into rubble. Humus had piled up, giving them purchase for their tent stakes. They lit a campfire, put on a field kettle, and began to boil stew out of beef jerky and hardtack. Vis insisted they gather around to sing a martial song to bolster their spirits.

There they were sitting around the fire singing when Lurk and Goth, misled by a tip from a local ghost who claimed to hate his descendants, came slogging down an alley and saw before them the barbarian camp they'd been looking for all day.

Lord Lurk came alive. "There they are! Fall upon them, men!"

The city folk felt absolutely no obligation to get in their way. Lurk's and Goth's men crashed into Ghouri's and Vis's, who shouted with fear and anger, retreated long enough to catch up their pikes, then waded in. It took only five minutes for Vis to realize who he was fighting. "Treachery! It's all a ruse! Lurk and Goth have led us here to kill us! Fight for your lives!"

They did. The men fought with pikes against shields; Vis hurled fire at Lurk, who made the pavement tremble and crack beneath him. Goth sent his wyverns against Ghouri's ghosts, but the ancestors trotted out a wyverneer of their own who sent the little monsters to hunt for rabbits—outside the city. Of course, Goth wasn't afraid of ghosts, so he drew his sword and attacked Ghouri hand to hand—but Ghouri proved to be just as skilled as he. Finally Goth slipped, Ghouri's sword slipped between his ribs, and a new ghost wavered in the air above the body, then took form. It shot up a thousand feet, took a look at what was happening, then plunged back at Ghouri, screaming, "You fool! They've misled us both, misled us into attacking one another!"

"Fool yourself!" cried the ghost of his sergeant. "If you two idiots hadn't brought us here, we'd still be alive!"

"Mind your tongue when you talk to your master!" Vis barked.

"Oh?" the sergeant asked. "What are you going to do—kill me?"

The increasing number of ghosts behind him shouted angry agreement and descended on their former master.

Those still living froze, watching, then turned on their living master with howls of vengeance.

Ghouri fled, but stepped in a pothole, tripped, and fell. In minutes, his ghost joined the mob assailing Vis's specter.

The troops of Magicians Borgen, Sechechs, and Espayic staggered into the large mall where Linden Tree Promenade met Centric Street. They pitched camp with the dragging steps and leaden arms of the exhausted, then collapsed on their blankets. For some of them, hunger was stronger than weariness, so a few cookfires blossomed in the dusk, though most managed to chew their beef jerky without benefit of boiling.

From an archway into a nearby courtyard, Longshanks watched with Solutre, Mira, Blaize, and Alea. "They won't split up! They just won't split up!"

"There has to be a way," Alea said.

"There is," Blaize said, face pale. "Assemble a hundred ghosts, tell them to make themselves look solid and only a little larger than normal, and have them charge the sleeping camp."

"Yessss!" Longshanks lifted his head. "The soldiers will strike and their blades will go right through—to cut into one another!"

"Ingenious," Alea agreed, "if we can trust the specters not to indulge in any of their usual haunting tricks."

"I'll have to lead the charge, of course," Blaize said, his face pale and strained.

"No!" Mira cried. "All their blades will stab at you!"

"There's no other way," Blaize said doggedly.

"There has to be!" Mira seized the chest of his tunic in both fists and shook him. "I won't let you turn into one more ghost! You have too much still to do here!"

"Do I?" Blaize asked, suddenly intense. "What?"

Mira stared into his eyes. Slowly, her hands relaxed, letting go of his tunic.

"Don't ask loaded questions," Alea snapped. "Mira, he's going to have to lead the charge. If you don't like it, set your pets to guard him."

Life came back into Mira's face, life and determination. "I will!"

• • •

Magician Sechechs looked up at the mass scream from the south side of the mall, then leaped to his feet shouting, "To arms! They're coming!"

Come they did, seeming merely mortal, though very odd. There were some seven feet tall and skinny as a rail, some three feet wide and five feet high, white hair, orange hair, green hair, white skins, mahogany skins, golden skins, blood red skins. Some wore robes, some tunics, some guards' uniforms; some bore staves, some bows, some strange pieces of pipe mounted in cross-bow stocks, and they yelled in a shrill, ululating howl that froze the soldiers in their tracks.

Borgen and Espayic tumbled from their tents right behind most of their soldiers—just in time for the barbarians to slam into them. They seemed to be everywhere in the encampment, swinging swords and battle axes and shooting flame from nozzles. Soldiers who could, ran; the rest howled in panic and swung back with the strength of desperation. The felt their blades strike home, they heard shrieks of pain, but the barbarians confronting them only laughed.

Finally Borgen realized what was happening. "They're ghosts!" he cried. "They can't hurt you! You're only striking each other!"

A few soldiers near him hesitated; none others could hear.

"There has to be a ghost-handler with them!" Borgen cried. "Find him and slay him! Then the ghosts will flee!"

"No, we won't, fatso!" one of the barbarians spat. He was a middle-aged ghost with fiery eyes and sideburns that suddenly burst into flame. "This is our city and we'll stay until you're all out of it!"

The air shimmered by him and the ghost of an old woman appeared, eyes wide in alarm. "They've found the village! Quickly, go defend it."

Lord Borgen laughed.

The old woman turned on him, snarling. "Villain! One of your ghosts found our descendants! You decoyed us here with your false encampment while fifty of your soldiers followed the specter to our village!"

17

Yes, and another fifty have run to join them while you've been attacking us here!" Borgen sneered. "Now we'll see how flesh and blood can stand up to my soldiers."

"For that you shall die!" the old woman spat.

"Die?" Borgen said, eyes mocking. "You're phantoms! Specters! Shadows! You can't hurt me!"

"Oh, yes, we can, my lord."

Borgen spun to see half a dozen men in his own livery marching toward him with ragged bloody holes in their tunics. One carried his head under his arm.

"You led us to our deaths for your pride," the bloody sergeant snarled. "We want revenge." His sword flashed.

Lord Borgen shivered even as he laughed. "I felt a chill sweep through me, nothing more."

"Indeed? All of you, now! Pierce him with your blades and hold them there!"

Borgen gasped in horror and pain as six separate chills seized his heart. He found himself staring into a face whose teeth grew into fangs and whose eyes turned to fire even as he watched. The nose and chin lengthened and he found himself staring into the blazing eyes of a man-wolf. For the first time since his early apprenticeship, he felt fear—but fear that grew and grew, making his heart hammer in panic. "Away!" he croaked. "You're only ghosts! Figments! Dreams! You can't . . . hurt . . ."

Then his heart stopped beating.

Minutes later, his own dead soldiers chased him around the battlefield with gloating laughter and ghostly spears.

Lord Espayic saw him pass and gasped. He turned on Sechechs. "You had the watch! You should have prevented this!"

"How?" Sechechs asked with contempt. "We were here to lull them while the ghost led our men to their camp, remember! Quickly, we must join them and make sure of our victory!"

Espayic started a hot retort, but Sechechs was already hurrying after his men, who were following a phantom, glad to be away from the mall and its ghosts. Espayic clamped his jaw shut, then called, "To me, men of mine!" and ran after Sechechs's men.

They burst into a plaza surrounded by tall buildings and centered by a circle of lawn with hoary old trees, several of which burned like giant torches. Beneath their leaves a desperate fight waged over the bodies of a dozen women and children. Borgen's men stood toe to toe with a line of barbarians, shouting in anger and clashing spearshaft against spear. Now and then a spearhead flashed and someone died shrieking. More barbarians came running with every minute.

The raw recruits tried to shy away, but Espayic and Sechechs drove them on with curses and fireballs. They crashed into the line of barbarians, which bowed, nearly broke, but steadied as dozens more like them came running to plug the holes where men and women dropped. Slowly, then, the bulge flattened.

Still the barbarians came running, more and more, but there were no more soldiers to join—they were all there already.

Lord Borgen's ghost came surging to the fight with dozens of dead magicians behind him, but his own dead men fought him with relish, sliding in and out of their former masters, confusing them horribly while legions of city ancestors came flocking to clear them out of the air.

"We can't win!" Espayic cried. "How did you think of this crazed idea?"

"I did my part!" Sechechs shouted. "I raised the alarm! What else would you have me do? I'm no ghost-leader!" He stabbed a finger at Borgen's shade. "There goes your ghost-handler! Blame him for your predicament!"

But Espayic saw something else. "Look! He's pointing! Borgen's pointing!"

Sechechs looked. "That knot of ghosts! They're clustered around that young phantom!" He seized the nearest living soldier and pointed. "Throw your spear into that crowd of ghosts as hard as you can!"

The man didn't think to object. He threw straight and true. Blaize cried out in pain and sank to his knees, trying to pull the spear from his thigh.

"He lives!" Sechechs shouted. "He's the one who has brought these phantoms upon us. Slay him, men, slay him!"

A dozen soldiers started toward the knot of ghosts, their spears leveled—until a dozen wyverns struck, breathing fire that lighted the night, talons reaching for the soldiers' faces.

"Away!" This Lord Sechechs could deal with. "Aroint thee! Begone!" He waved his hands to dispel the flock.

They let go of the soldiers, then rose ten feet—but Sechechs felt a mind warring with his, felt a tugging at the invisible strands that bound the wyverns to him. Suddenly a face seemed to glow over the battle, the face of a young woman, a yard high and burning with anger, beautiful in wrath. In sheer surprise Sechechs loosed his hold—and a wyvern plunged toward him with jaws open and claws out. He died with talons in his heart and teeth in his throat.

Espayic needed no second warning. "Away!" he cried. "Down the avenue! Retreat!"

He led the way. A score of soldiers broke free and followed him, but most of their comrades remained behind.

By the time Espayic passed out of the city and threw himself gasping on the grass of the fields outside, he had only half a dozen guards left. Looking back toward the ghost-fires that played about the towers, he shuddered, amazed that so many could die.

Some had. Most had not. Gar and Alea had many more recruits the next day.

Mira plunged through the mob of cheering, dancing ghosts and threw herself on Blaize, winding a length of cloth around the gash in his thigh. "You're wounded! They've hurt you!"

"They only sliced meat." Blaize sat up and caught her hand, grinning. "There isn't enough blood to be dangerous. I probably won't even limp a month from now."

Mira stared at him, transfixed, then threw her arms around him with a glad cry.

All over the battlefield, barbarians were tending wounded soldiers. Longshanks looked on, puzzled. "Those barbarians were real! There were more than ghosts here, and there are twenty times as many of them as there are Corbies!"

"You did have a little more help than you realized."

The barbarian looked up at the ghost towering over him. Beside him, Alea said slowly, "Longshanks, may I introduce you to a friend of ours—Conn."

"And a friend of mine." Conn gestured as a lithe, well-muscled man with a pocked face came up. "This is Hengst, war leader of the Ansax Clan of Cumber City, here with warriors from all its six clans!"

Longshanks stared for a moment, then stepped forward, palm raised. "Thank you for kind rescue!"

"Our pleasure." Hengst pressed his palm against Longshanks's. "Conn here came to us a month ago and started teaching us about the Tao."

"I wondered where you'd gone," Alea said to Conn. He grinned in return.

"When a friend of Conn's sent word through a chain of ghosts that the magicians were marching against you, we realized that all the cities are connected, in the magicians' minds if in no other way, and that what they would do to you, they would do to us all—so we came to help out."

"I'm very glad you did," Longshanks said fervently.

"You seem to have really taken to the idea of sending messages through a chain of ghosts," Alea said to Conn.

"Your friend Gar started more that he knew, when he invented that ghost-to-ghost hookup," Conn said. He turned to Longshanks. "I have other friends. Here's one."

Ranulf's ghost came drifting up, followed by a wiry barbarian woman almost as tall as Longshanks with hair roached high and colored blue.

"Longshanks and Hengst, this is my friend Ranulf," Conn said.

"And this is *my* friend Dramout." Ranulf gestured to the barbarian. "She's the war leader of the clan of Brandy from Vetarna City."

"Two other cities come to help us!" Longshanks said, awed, as he pressed palms with Dramout.

"We're all caught in the web of the Tao," Dramout said, "so we might as well stand up for one another."

"We shall, if ever you are attacked," Longshanks promised.

Gar came up behind Alea. She smiled at him. "Things seem to have worked out even better than you planned."

"Yes, except for the people who died." Gar's face was set in grim lines.

Alea sighed. "People would have died in the magicians' battles if you hadn't come here. Women and children would have died from famine or the lords' punishments. Now, though, the cities will spread the Way throughout the countryside, and the magicians will have to agree to a code of ethics or be drowned by sheer numbers. Every warrior who died here today has saved at lest a thousand lives in the future."

"I wish I could be sure of that," Gar said, his face haunted. "I wish I could be sure they thought it worth their lives."

"Ask them." Alea nodded toward a cluster of glowing forms—warriors' spirits rising from their dead bodies, looking about them dazed and disbelieving at the loud welcomes of the ancestral ghosts who crowded around them.

"If you have any doubts, ask them," Alea said again. "This is the one planet where you can, after all."

The surviving lords, chastened by the example of the battle, signed a treaty and marched their soldiers out of the city, well aware that their movements would be monitored by a chain of ghosts reporting their deeds. The city clans bound up their wounded, buried their dead, then held a banquet for their new allies, who stayed a day or two to agree on ways to stay in touch in the future, even to begin work toward an intercity council. Then they, too, went home, and the next morning, Alea and Gar came out atop the tallest building with Mira and Blaize, who stood arm in arm, still dazed and delighted by what had happened between them.

"It's up to you two now," Gar said quietly. "This is only a beginning, you know."

"Yes, we do," Mira said, large-eyed. "All the cities have to learn the Way and join together. Then we can start to pressure the magicians to stop exploiting their serfs—but it will take a long time."

"A life's work," Blaize agreed.

"Is it worth your lives?" Alea asked.

The two smiled into one another's eyes and nodded. "As long as you're with me," Mira said.

"And you won't mind if I'm a magician?" Blaize teased.

"Can you be a good magician?" Mira challenged.

"As long as you're with me," Blaize answered.

"Don't try to make the clans accept you as leaders," Gar cautioned. "It's enough to be their friends and teach the Way. Wait for them to come to you for advice."

Mira nodded. "We'll just be sages."

"We'll lead by example," Blaize promised.

"Good enough, then." Gar smiled, pressing their hands. "Good-bye and good luck."

"Good-bye?" Mira stared. "How can you say good-bye on top of a tower?"

"Here comes our chariot." Alea pointed upward. "Stand against the elevator motorhouse and don't be afraid."

Mira and Blaize retreated to the shelter of the blockhouse that stood in the middle of the building's flat roof, then watched, spellbound and disbelieving, as the great golden ship swung lower and lower, hovered, then extended legs to the rooftop and lowered a ramp. Alea and Gar climbed it, stopped at the top, and turned to wave.

Mira and Blaize waved back, watching wide-eyed as their friends went on up into their ship. Then Mira pointed. "Look! What is that strange creature that follows them?"

Blaize frowned. "What strange creature? I saw nothing."

"Saw nothing?" Mira stared up at him. "What should you have seen?"

"I . . . I don't know," Blaize said slowly. "I thought I knew, but I don't."

Mira nodded. "I thought I remembered something, but it must have been a ghost of the mind."

"Well, there are enough of them here." Blaize smiled and kissed her, then said, "Come, let's go down to join our friends. It's cold up here."

"As soon as they leave." Mira turned to watch the great golden ship as it rose, hovered over the building, then shot upward, rising higher and higher until it was only a speck in the dawn sky, then gone. Her head was tilted back, eyes filled with brand-new sunlight. She smiled up at Blaize. "All right. We can go back now."

"Not quite yet," Blaize said, and kissed her.

Aboard the ship, Alea came out of her suite in a soft white robe, towel wound about her head like a long-tailed turban, and collapsed into an automatic chair with a sigh. She let it adjust to her contours, enjoying the sensation as she remembered that only two years before, that same feeling had scared the daylights out of her. She stretched out a hand to the tall glass beside her, sipped the drink, then set it back and smiled at Gar, who sat across from her, similarly scrubbed and robed. "That seems to have worked out well after all," Alea said.

"Yes, it does," Gar agreed. "Care to try again?"

"Yes, I think so," Alea said, "but not right away." She frowned. "Do you really think those ghosts were real?"

In the hold below her, a round-headed cat-faced alien lifted her head, gazing up as though she could see through the deck to the woman above, then lowered her nose and tucked it into her tail. Evanescent sighed, pleased that she had only needed to nudge a little here and there during the final battle. That native woman had surprised her, though, there at the last—her mind reading had been much more acute than she'd shown before, actually glimpsing the alien climbing up the ship's ramp, and Evanescent had needed to do a little quick memory erasing before she had gone into the ship.

Still, it was done, and well done. It had all been very amusing, strengthening telepaths and hindering ghosts—but it had been surprisingly wearying, too. Evanescent yawned and composed herself for a month or two of sleep.